A mu every inch o covered in s

"Enough!" Logan hollered, collapsing on the embankment, sides heaving with laughter.

Fletcher fell down next to him, chuckling. "Man, I haven't heard you laugh like that in a long time."

His friend's words sobered Logan. He struggled to catch his breath.

A long silence stretched between the men, then Fletcher spoke. "You think I should have given Sandi a second chance—for Danny's sake?"

The two men were thirty years old, their birthdays two weeks apart in July. They'd been friends since kindergarten and had stuck by each other through thick and thin. Through divorce and death.

"Did Sandi want a second chance?" Logan asked.

"No."

"Did you want a second chance with her?"

"No." Fletcher released a loud gust of air from his lungs. "If Bethany had cheated on you, would you have divorced her?"

"I don't know." Logan wished Bethany had cheated, instead of dying. "We're a real pair, aren't we?"

Dear Reader,

I love writing about cowboys and what a treat it's been writing not one but two cowboy Christmas stories. In *A Cowboy Christmas* best friends Logan Taylor and Fletcher McFadden have each recently struggled through hard times and they're hesitant to give love a try again. Logan must find the courage to move on after his wife's death and Fletcher struggles with dating and single fatherhood after his recent divorce.

Christmas isn't just a holiday for presents and parties. It's also a time for forgiveness and new beginnings. I hope you enjoy reading how Logan and Fletcher find their happy-ever-afters with the women they least expected to.

May the spirit of Christmas fill your heart and bring many blessings to you and your loved ones.

For more information on my books visit www.marinthomas.com. For up-to-date news on Harlequin American Romance authors and their books visit www.harauthors.blogspot.com.

Happy reading!

Marin

A Cowboy Christmas
MARIN THOMAS

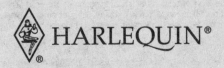

HARLEQUIN®

TORONTO • NEW YORK • LONDON
AMSTERDAM • PARIS • SYDNEY • HAMBURG
STOCKHOLM • ATHENS • TOKYO • MILAN • MADRID
PRAGUE • WARSAW • BUDAPEST • AUCKLAND

Recycling programs
for this product may
not exist in your area.

ISBN-13: 978-0-373-75292-8

A COWBOY CHRISTMAS

Copyright © 2009 by Harlequin Books S.A.

The publisher acknowledges the copyright holder of the individual works as follows:

A CHRISTMAS BABY
Copyright © 2009 by Brenda Smith-Beagley

MARRY ME, COWBOY
Copyright © 2009 by Brenda Smith-Beagley

www.eHarlequin.com

Printed in U.S.A.

CONTENTS

ABOUT THE AUTHOR

Marin Thomas grew up in Janesville, Wisconsin. She attended the University of Arizona in Tucson on a Division I basketball scholarship. In 1986 she graduated with a B.A. in radio-television and married her college sweetheart in a five-minute ceremony in Las Vegas. Marin was inducted in May 2005 into the Janesville Sports Hall of Fame for her basketball accomplishments. Even though she now calls Chicago home, she's a living testament to the old adage "You can take the girl out of the small town, but you can't take the small town out of the girl." Marin's heart still lies in small-town life, which she loves to write about in her books.

Books by Marin Thomas

HARLEQUIN AMERICAN ROMANCE
1024—THE COWBOY AND THE BRIDE
1050—DADDY BY CHOICE
1079—HOMEWARD BOUND
1124—AARON UNDER CONSTRUCTION*
1148—NELSON IN COMMAND*
1165—SUMMER LOVIN'
       "The Preacher's Daughter"
1175—RYAN'S RENOVATION*
1184—FOR THE CHILDREN**
1200—IN A SOLDIER'S ARMS**
1224—A COAL MINER'S WIFE**
1236—THE COWBOY AND THE ANGEL
1253—COWBOY'S PROMISE
1271—SAMANTHA'S COWBOY

*The McKade Brothers
**Hearts of Appalachia

A CHRISTMAS BABY

To my son, Thomas—
congratulations on your high school graduation!
I'm proud of the wonderful young man you've become.
Whatever path you choose in life I hope it brings you
happiness, joy and most of all love.

Go get 'em, Dude!

Chapter One

"How the hell did your bull end up in my mud bog?" Logan Taylor asked his best friend and neighbor, Fletcher McFadden. Fletcher had called Logan a half hour ago requesting help. Luckily Logan had his cell phone with him in the barn where he'd been mucking out stalls.

"Danny left the gate open again." Danny was Fletcher's seven-year-old son. The kid was a handful.

Logan didn't comment on the boy's carelessness. Danny was going through a rough patch after Fletcher and the boy's mother divorced. Come to think about it, all three of them—Danny, Fletcher and himself—had seen better days. "I brought a sling," Logan said. He'd also loaded a few hay bales into the truck bed. He'd spread the hay around the edge of the bog to help the bull gain its footing after the animal was freed. He motioned to Fletcher who stood knee-deep in muck. "What do you plan to do—push the bull end over end until he rolls out of there?"

"Ha, ha. Hurry up, hoss. My feet are numb."

Logan tossed two ends of the sling through the air.

A warm spell had ushered in the first week of December, but a chill hung in the early-morning air and white clouds puffed from Fletcher's mouth as he struggled to work the harness beneath the ten inches of space between the bull's belly and the mud.

"You ever think about fixing this bog?" Fletcher grunted.

Granted, Logan should have filled the mud hole long ago. The problem was he didn't give a crap about much anymore. After Bethany died everything had lost its urgency. He was marking time. Waiting for something to change his life. Waiting for…just waiting.

Although Fletcher had his share of troubles recovering from a divorce and raising a son, he'd tried to drag Logan back into the world of the living after Bethany's death. Logan appreciated his friend's concern but preferred a solitary existence.

"All set." Fletcher flung the ends of the harness over the bull's body and Logan secured them to the trailer hitch on his truck.

"I can't lose this bull to a broken leg," Fletcher warned.

The McFaddens raised some of the best breeding bulls in Texas. "How much is he worth?" Logan asked.

"So much he ain't for sale."

Logan removed a pair of wire cutters from his pocket and opened the bales in the truck bed. After tossing the hay along the edge of the bog he hopped in his truck.

"Nice and easy!" Fletcher hollered.

Nice and easy was the only way to pull a two-thousand-pound hunk of beef from a muddy hole. Logan pressed the accelerator and the truck's tires dug into the earth. He checked his side mirror. Fletcher had his shoulder jammed against the bull's side, trying to coax it to move its legs.

The animal slowly toppled onto its side. With steady pressure on the gas pedal, Logan moved the truck a few feet forward. For a second the bull sank beneath the mud, only the whites of its eyes visible. Logan gave the truck a little more gas and the animal's head emerged.

"Keep going," Fletcher said. "He's almost to the edge."

The diesel truck engine groaned in protest, but finally the bull reached solid ground. Logan dragged its body a few more feet until the bull lay on the hay, then he cut the engine and rushed to untie the harness from the hitch before the animal became tangled.

The bull's sides heaved with exertion but after Logan slapped its hind quarters, the animal scrambled to its feet, slipping once but remaining upright. He trotted off, bellowing in disgust.

"You coming out of there?"

"I can't feel my legs," Fletcher complained.

Logan grinned.

"Give me your hand."

"Sorry, buddy. No can do." Logan wasn't about to risk falling into the bog. "Here." He threw one end of the harness and Fletcher snatched it mid-air, then Logan tied the other end to the trailer hitch.

"Take it easy. These are my favorite boots."

Not for long, buddy. Logan hopped into the front seat and revved the engine. "Hang on!" As soon as Fletcher tightened his grip, Logan pressed the gas— hard—and the truck exploded forward. Fletcher flew through the air, sans boots, and landed on his belly at the edge of the bog. When he tried to stand, Logan hit the gas again and dragged Fletcher through the hay.

"God damn it, Logan!" Fletcher released the ends of the harness and attempted to stand. His feet slid out from under him and he went down a second time.

"You look like the scarecrow from the *Wizard of Oz*," Logan called out the truck window.

"Think that's funny, eh?"

Logan hopped out of the truck and went to help his friend stand. Fletcher grasped Logan's wrist and yanked. Logan stumbled forward, bumping Fletcher, and the two men toppled over like felled trees into the muck.

From there things went downhill faster than a California mudslide.

"You shithead." Fletcher flung a clump of mud at Logan's chest.

"You would have done the same thing if it had been me standing in that bog." Logan landed a mud ball against the side of Fletcher's head.

A mud-slinging battle ensued until every inch of their clothing was covered in smelly muck. "Enough!" Logan hollered, collapsing on the embankment, sides heaving with laughter.

Fletcher fell down next to him, chuckling. "Man, I haven't heard you laugh like that in a hell of a long time."

His friend's words sobered Logan. He struggled to catch his breath. Now that the fun was over, his body felt chilled.

A long silence stretched between the men, then Fletcher spoke.

"You think I should have given Sandi a second chance—for Danny's sake?"

The two men were thirty years old, their birthdays two weeks apart in July. They'd been friends since kindergarten and had stuck by each other through thick and thin. Through divorce and death.

"Did Sandi want a second chance?" Logan asked.

"No."

"Did you want a second chance with her?" Logan asked.

"No." Fletcher released a loud gust of air from his lungs. "If Bethany had cheated on you, would you have divorced her?"

"I don't know." Logan wished Bethany had cheated. Pretty damned difficult to work out marriage troubles with a dead spouse. "Stop beating yourself up over the divorce. Danny needs time to adjust is all."

"You're probably right." Fletcher punched Logan in the arm. "I met a woman named Daisy on MySpace." Fletcher had set up a MySpace page months ago and had tried to persuade Logan to join in the fun. He'd refused.

"Daisy? What the hell kind of name is that?"

"Everyone uses fake names on MySpace," Fletcher said.

"What's your handle?"

"Leonard. Lenny for short." He grinned.

"Yeah, well, good luck with your little flower."

They crawled to their feet. "Thanks for helping with the bull," Fletcher said.

"Anytime."

Hobbling sock-footed toward his truck, Fletcher said over his shoulder. "I'm throwing steaks on the grill tonight. You're welcome for supper."

"Think I'll pass."

"If you change your mind, we're eating at six." Fletcher honked and drove off.

Logan watched the blue horizon swallow his friend's truck. West Texas was flat and barren and not a tree in sight. Most people considered this part of the Longhorn State the ugliest but the vast emptiness matched the way he felt on the inside.

Keeping to himself might be easier on the heart and mind, but it sure was damned lonely on the soul.

LOGAN'S FOOT ITCHED like the dickens, which meant only one thing—bad luck headed his way.

After helping Fletcher rescue the bull from the mud bog a week ago Monday, there hadn't been much excitement in Logan's day-to-day routine. The red Ford Focus hatchback winding its way along the ribbon of ranch road was about to change all that.

He slunk into the shadows inside the barn doors. He'd rather go another round with a mud-bogged bull than face the woman heading in his direction.

Three months had passed since he'd gone on a bender and had himself a hog-killin' time at Billie's Roadhouse ten miles south of Junket. When the local hairdresser had strolled into the honky-tonk, Logan's boot heel had been planted on the brass rail long enough to take root.

If Cassidy Ortiz hadn't left him a note the following morning, he would have speculated the rest of his years about who had worn the sultry scent that had clung to his pillow. Until now he'd been successful in avoiding the lady—not an easy task in a town the size of Junket, Texas. Population two-hundred-sixty-nine.

The hatchback stopped next to his truck parked in front of the house.

Turn around and leave. He slunk deeper into the shadows.

The car door opened.

No. No.

A cowboy boot appeared, then a jean-clad leg. No need for a jacket since the morning chill had worn off. A sweater would do—like the tight one that hugged her breasts when she reached across the front seat for... A dish?

Object in her hands forgotten, he zeroed in on her curves. How did any man, even a drunk one, forget a body like Cassidy's? A tightening below his belt buckle suggested that certain parts of his anatomy had no trouble recalling her.

A wind gust blew her long midnight-colored hair against her face, blocking his view of her high cheek-bones and dark, slanted eyes. She bumped the car door shut with her hip and strolled along the sidewalk. The swish-sway of her fanny reminded him that the stylist had nothing in common with Bethany, who'd been a small-boned, frail blonde.

Cassidy knocked on the front door.

Nobody's home.

Another round of knocking. Then she crossed to the front window by the porch swing and peered inside.

Persistent woman.

Right then Twister loped around the corner of the house. Logan didn't know who was more surprised— the deaf German shepherd when he spotted the visitor or Cassidy when the dog snarled. Twister was all bark and no bite, so Logan didn't intervene.

She tossed a piece of whatever was on the plate to the dog. Twister caught the treat midair, then wagged his tail as if it were a checkered flag at a stock car race. Cassidy inched toward the porch steps, pausing every few feet to fling another morsel at Twister.

If you don't go out there and speak with her, she'll stop by again.

He'd lock the entrance gate off the main road.

She'll call.

He wouldn't answer the phone.

What if she's got something important to say?

If it was that important why had she waited all this time to come around? *Aw, hell.* He might as well get this over with. He made it halfway to the house before she noticed him. Her smile knocked him sideways, but he didn't break stride. "Cassidy."

"Hi, Logan. I was about to leave. I thought you weren't home." Twister growled and she jumped.

Logan stomped his boot on the ground and the dog immediately quieted. At Cassidy's raised eyebrow he explained. "Twister's deaf. He wandered into the ranch yard a few years ago after a tornado blew through." Logan shrugged. "Vet thinks the noise from the storm ruptured his eardrums."

"Oh, how sad."

"Is there a reason you stopped by?" Logan cleared his throat and she flinched at his rudeness.

Damn. He hadn't meant to sound like an ass. His social skills were rusty, considering he mostly kept to himself—except for that night at Billie's Roadhouse.

He blamed his behavior that day on the stupid drugstore window display in town. Who the hell put up Christmas decorations in September? Logan had snapped when he'd spotted the twinkling lights on the artificial tree and the toy train that circled the base. The cozy scene had dredged up memories he wanted no part of.

To run from the recollections of that fateful day just before Christmas the previous year he'd headed to the nearest honky-tonk. After three beers Bethany's memory had remained as vivid as ever and he'd switched to tequila shots. When Cassidy had strolled into the bar he'd been too drunk to hit the ground with his hat in three tries. No match for a pretty face and a sympathetic ear, he'd hadn't objected when Cassidy had offered to drive him home. Logan shook his head as he realized she was staring at him.

"I made you—" she glanced at the plate covered in green plastic wrap, then shoved it at him "—Christmas cookies."

Cookies? They'd had sex. One time. Maybe two. All that mattered was their *relationship* had lasted less than twenty-four hours. He hadn't called her the next day. Or the next. Or the next day after that. And Cassidy hadn't contacted him, leading him to believe that what had happened that night between them was over. Finished. Terminated.

Done.

The plate nudged his chest like a big fat finger poking his breastbone. There was only part of one cookie—a frosted reindeer head complete with antlers and a red nose—left. He gripped the dish. "Christmas is three weeks away." And he intended to allow the day to pass without any fanfare.

"Mom and I got a head start on our holiday baking."

She laughed nervously, and her breasts jiggled. He resisted the urge to rub his eyeballs, which suddenly felt too big for their sockets.

"There were a dozen cookies—" she glanced at the reindeer head "—but I gave the others to the dog, so he wouldn't attack," she said.

"He acts mean, but he won't bite."

"If you say so." Cassidy flashed a quick smile, showing off her pretty white teeth and full lower lip.

He really needed her to leave. When she didn't… "I'm busy. If that's all you—"

"Wait!" She stepped in front of him, blocking his getaway route. His damned foot itched again and a sense of foreboding settled in his bones like a bad case of rheumatism. He brushed past her and had almost escaped when…

"Logan, I'm pregnant."

The heel of his boot caught the edge of the step, sending him sprawling onto the porch. The cookie plate flew from his hand, bounced off the front door, then slid to a stop under the swing. Twister vaulted over Logan's body and snarfed up the broken reindeer head.

"Oh, my God. Are you all right?" Cassidy rushed to his side.

Shrugging off her touch, he crawled to his feet. His shins stung and his chin hurt like hell where he'd banged it against the step. But the worst pain settled in his chest—a tight squeezing pressure that threatened to suffocate him.

"Please listen, Logan."

His legs wouldn't move—his traitorous feet had frozen in place.

"Bethany mentioned to me how badly you'd both wanted a child…" Cassidy ceased rambling and for a moment Logan believed he might catch his breath, then she continued and his lungs pinched closed again. "I know how devastated you were—" her voice dropped to a whisper "—that Bethany was carrying your baby when she died."

Lack of oxygen numbed his brain and Cassidy's words sounded garbled as if water had flooded his ears.

"I…" She paused, then rushed on. "Plan to keep the baby."

Unable to trust himself to say anything appropriate, he remained stone-faced. After a tense stare-down, she spun on her boot heel and trotted to the hatchback. The car sped off, leaving a cloud of dust lingering in the air and Logan with a knot the size of Texas in his chest.

DON'T YOU DARE CRY.

Cassidy stopped the car at the entrance to the Bar T Ranch and rested her head against the steering wheel.

She'd put off telling Logan about the baby for three months because she didn't want to say anything until the risky first trimester was over. She'd expected the cowboy to be shocked by the news, but not so…so cold. Even now the memory of his flat stare left her shaky.

Her eyes watered and this time a tear dribbled down her cheek.

Logan still mourned Bethany—the love of his life. The girl he'd dated all through high school and had married after graduation. Like clockwork Bethany had scheduled a haircut once a month when Cassidy opened her salon five years ago. Not long after, Bethany had confided in Cassidy about her miscarriages. They'd mourned each time the young woman had lost a baby and celebrated every time the home pregnancy test showed a plus sign.

What broke Cassidy's heart was Bethany's teary confession that all she'd ever wanted was to give Logan a child. Then when Bethany had finally succeeded in carrying a baby through the first trimester, she'd been killed in a car accident on the way to a doctor's appointment in Midland.

No one, no matter how pure or goodhearted, avoided life's cruel twists and turns.

A tiny part of Cassidy had hoped for a hint of excitement from Logan. After all, he'd wanted a baby for years. *You're such a fool. He wanted Bethany's baby—not yours.*

Well, she possessed enough enthusiasm for both of them. Cassidy would be twenty-eight in January and she had always wanted to marry and have a family. Her situation with Logan might not be ideal, but a baby was a blessing no matter how the child was conceived, and she was determined that Logan's cool reaction wouldn't dampen her joy.

Lifting her foot from the brake, she drove east toward the trailer park on the outskirts of Junket where she and her mother lived. She suspected Logan wished Mr. Claus was in the business of granting "do-overs." If so, he'd probably ask jolly old St. Nick to erase that September night she'd strolled into the bar to let her hair down after a stressful day of caring for her mother.

Billie's Roadhouse was known for its live bands and big dance floor. That particular evening Cassidy had been on the hunt for a cowboy to dance with into the wee hours of the morning.

Dance with—not have sex with.

When she'd spotted Logan drinking shots at the bar she'd gone over to say hello. The silly, drunken grin he'd flashed had put her dancing plans on the back burner. The bartender had held out Logan's truck keys, assuming she'd arrived to haul his inebriated carcass home. She could have said no. She could have phoned Logan's friend, Fletcher, to come get him.

But you didn't.

Her and Logan's fate had been sealed the moment she'd grasped the truck keys from the bartender. Afterward, she'd spent weeks making up excuses for her behavior that night.

Logan had been too drunk to drive.

Logan had needed to eat, and she'd insisted on cooking him a meal.

Logan needed to sober up, so she'd helped him shower.

Logan needed a babysitter—in case he'd vomited—so she'd rested on the bed with him.

Her intent had been to slip away before dawn, but then he'd called out Bethany's name in his sleep and Cassidy had woken to his hand on her breast, his eyes shimmering with grief and pain. Logan had hit rock bottom and Cassidy hadn't had the heart or willpower to turn him away.

Forcing the memories aside, she flipped on the blinker and entered the Shady Acres Trailer Park. She could count on one hand the number of shade trees throughout the twenty acre patch of flat Texas dirt. The owner of the property had invested little money in landscaping. Most of the park's tenants struggled to make their rent payment and what extra money they earned went toward food and clothing, not flowers or bushes.

Years ago Cassidy's mother had planted a cherry tree in the small yard alongside their trailer. Today the tree stood twenty-five feet high and in April its pink blossoms added a touch of beauty to the stark neighborhood. Best of all, the tree provided much needed shade for the aluminum shed Cassidy used as a hair studio.

At half-past one in the afternoon the kids were in school and the neighborhood was quiet. She slowed the car as it passed over the first of two speed bumps and noticed the Millers had strung Christmas lights on their trailer. Cassidy took great pride in being the first Shady Acres tenant to decorate for Christmas. She'd made a habit of hanging her lights over Thanksgiving weekend. But her mother's temperament had been more difficult than usual this holiday and Cassidy hadn't had the energy to dig through boxes of decorations. After she parked next to the single-wide and got out of the car, her neighbor greeted her.

"Hello, Cassidy."

"Hi, Betty."

Betty's *cousin,* Alice, appeared. "Sonja's been inside the whole time you were gone."

"Mom's frosting Christmas cookies. We'll bring a dozen over later today."

The little old ladies had claimed to be related when they'd moved into the park eight years ago, but no cousins Cassidy knew held hands like her neighbors. She didn't care what kind of relationship the women had. After Cassidy's mother had been officially diagnosed with Alzheimer's two years ago, Betty and Alice had offered to keep an eye on Sonja when Cassidy ran errands. She owed her neighbors a debt of gratitude.

When Cassidy entered the trailer, she found her mother exactly where she'd left her—sitting at the card table in front of the TV. Pieces of broken cookie littered the tabletop and smears of colored frosting marred her mother's blouse.

"Who's that?" her mother called, gaze glued to the TV.

"It's me, Mom." She approached the table and inspected the cookies. "I like that one." She pointed at the snowflake coated with an inch of silver-colored sugar crystals.

"I made that for you." Her mother smiled.

"Mmm." Cassidy took a bite and choked on the sweetness. When her mother's attention drifted to her favorite game show, Cassidy went into the kitchen, tossed the rest of the cookie into the trash and checked the clock. She had fifteen minutes to prepare for Mrs. Wilson's hair appointment. "I'll be in the salon if you need me, Mom."

Cassidy went outside to the shed, propping the doors open with potted plants. She'd saved her paychecks from a chain hair salon she'd worked at in Midland for two years to buy the aluminum building and beauty-shop equipment. Then she'd paid a fortune for a plumber to hook up a sink. She used extension cords and an outlet strip to plug in the hair dryers and curling irons and the two lamps she'd set on end tables. Between her mother's social security checks and Cassidy's income from styling hair they managed to make ends meet.

Her mother had been forced into early retirement because of health problems and so far Cassidy hadn't had to touch a dime of her mother's savings—money Sonja had set aside during the twenty-five years she'd worked at the fertilizer factory between Junket and Midland. Cassidy would use that money to put her mother in a home when the time arrived that she needed constant care.

Mrs. Wilson pulled up in her Lincoln Town Car. "Right on time, Mabel." The retired schoolteacher was never late.

Mabel set her purse on the loveseat Cassidy had found in a secondhand store the previous summer. "How's Sonja?"

"Mom's doing well." She refrained from discussing her mother's worsening condition. If people learned how quickly Sonja's disease was progressing they'd encourage Cassidy to put her in a home sooner rather than later.

"Go a little darker on the rinse, dear. I don't want the color to fade before the Smith's party on the eighteenth."

After months of pleading with the older woman to experiment with a different hair color, Cassidy had given up. Mabel insisted on using old-fashioned blue hair rinse. Cassidy draped a cape across Mabel's shoulders. "How's Buford?" Her husband had retired from the state highway patrol this past summer.

"He's being an ass."

"What's he gone and done now?" Listening to her customers vent was part of the job. Cassidy mixed the hair color, then cleaned her trimming scissors while Mabel droned on.

"He's refusing to allow Harriet and her new husband to join us for Christmas dinner."

"I thought Buford liked your sister."

"It's husband number four he hates."

Harriet exchanged husbands as often as women switched lipstick colors.

"Mitchell's a lawyer." Mabel twisted in the chair and said, "You know how much Buford hates lawyers."

Poor Buford. He'd earned a reputation of having the highest percentage of nonconvictable arrests during his tenure on the force. Cassidy changed the subject. "How do you like teaching Sunday school?"

"Aside from a few rambunctious boys the kids are well-behaved. They need a substitute teacher for the first-grade class if you're interested."

"Not right now, Mabel." Cassidy had stopped attending church months ago after her mother had stood up in front of the entire congregation and announced that if she didn't go to the bathroom right then she'd pee her pants.

While Mabel chatted about the children's holiday play, Cassidy slipped on a pair of latex gloves and worked the blue dye into Mabel's hair, then set the timer for an extra ten minutes and placed a magazine in her lap. "I need to check on Mom."

When Cassidy entered the trailer and peeked around the kitchen doorway, she discovered her mother fast asleep in the recliner. Relieved, Cassidy poured a glass of lemonade for her customer, then returned to the shed.

"Thank you, dear." After a sip, Mabel said, "I hear there's a new doctor in Midland who specializes in brain problems like your mother's."

"Really?" Old people were afraid if they spoke the word *Alzheimer's* out loud they'd contract the dreaded disease.

"I'll find out his name before my next hair appointment."

"That'd be great, thanks." Her mother's insurance didn't cover experimental tests or medicines. Cassidy had spent hours on the phone with insurance representatives, each call ending with "I wish there was more we could do, but unfortunately…"

The timer dinged and Cassidy rinsed the dye from Mabel's hair. Next, she trimmed the ends, then retrieved a pink plastic tub of rollers from the storage cabinet. She'd put in the final roller when a truck pulled alongside the Lincoln.

"Why, it's Logan Taylor," Mabel said.

The cowboy sported the same somber expression he'd worn earlier in the day when Cassidy had stopped by his ranch.

"How long have you been cutting his hair?" The gleam in Mabel's eyes warned Cassidy not to say too much, lest she give the woman the idea that she and Logan had a thing going—which they didn't.

"Logan isn't one of my clients." Mabel opened her mouth, but Cassidy cut her off. "Time for the dryer."

"Hello, Logan." Mabel wiggled her fingers in the air.

Feeling Mabel's eyes on her, Cassidy offered a weak smile.

Logan cut through the yard, stopping outside the shed doors. "Mrs. Wilson," he greeted the older woman. Then his gaze shifted to Cassidy. "Do you have a minute?"

"Sure." She tucked Mabel's head under the dryer, flipped the switch to high and lowered the hood. Hoping the noise would drown out whatever Logan had to say, she stepped outside the shed.

His shadow fell over her like a dark, menacing storm cloud. He didn't speak, which gave her a chance to study him—shaggy, dark hair, cheeks covered in beard stubble and dark smudges beneath his brown eyes. Why hadn't she noticed his unkempt appearance earlier?

Because you had other things on your mind.

"About that night…" He removed his Stetson and twirled it around his middle finger. "I had too much to drink—"

"That's why I drove you home." That was the truth—sort of.

The cowboy hat spun faster. "So…did I or did you…"

"Neither actually." He hadn't asked her to stay nor had he asked her to leave. She hadn't offered to stay nor had she offered to leave. "It just happened."

Her heart ached at the abject misery in the man's eyes. The fact that he failed to remember their lovemaking should have hurt or angered her, but she felt only sympathy for him.

"I thought you should know about the baby." She sucked in a quiet breath. "In case you wanted to be involved in the pregnancy." She'd hoped, prayed, fantasized that Logan would step up to the plate and be a father to their child, regardless of his feelings toward her.

His gaze wandered around the yard. "Are you…"

The words were barely a whisper and Cassidy had trouble hearing above the hum of the hair dryer. "What did you say?"

Right then Mabel shut off the dryer at the same time Logan raised his voice. "Are you sure the baby's mine?"

Mabel gasped.
Cassidy stared in shock.
Logan groaned.
Oops. The cat was out of the bag.

Chapter Two

The blood drained from Cassidy's face, leaving her skin as white as the siding on the trailer. She swayed to the left, then to the right. Fearing she'd topple, Logan grabbed her arm and hauled her to the trailer steps a few feet away. "Put your head between your knees." He pressed his hand against the back of her neck, ignoring the silky texture of her hair.

"Oh, dear. You're feeling poorly." Mrs. Wilson rushed to Cassidy's side, her plastic cape flapping in the air.

"I'm fine," Cassidy mumbled between her legs.

Logan's nose curled at the smell of ammonia rising from the older woman's head. No wonder Cassidy felt sick—breathing toxic fumes all day.

"Listen, dear. I'll leave and—"

"Give me a minute, Mabel."

"If you're sure…" Mrs. Wilson retreated to the shed and ducked her head beneath the dryer.

"I'll get you some water." Logan stepped past Cassidy and entered the trailer's kitchen, then searched the cupboards for a drinking glass.

"Cassidy? Are you makin' all that racket?"

Crap. "It's Logan Taylor, Mrs. Ortiz." He poked his head around the doorway. "Cassidy needs a drink of water."

"Oh." The older woman glanced across the room. "I don't know where Cassidy is."

"She's outside." He resumed his search.

A few seconds later…"Cassidy? You makin' all that racket in there?"

"Logan Taylor, ma'am." He wondered if Cassidy's mother knew about the baby. Logan found a glass, ran the cold tap, then headed outside. "Here." He handed Cassidy the drink, before retreating to the bottom of the steps.

"I don't bite." She flashed a crooked smile.

If not for the pasty color of her complexion, he'd have two-stepped toward his truck and gotten the heck out of Dodge. "Do you need me to take you to a doctor?"

The smile vanished. "I don't *need* you to do anything, Logan."

Fearing his presence upset her, he said, "Maybe we should talk later."

Cassidy glanced at Mrs. Wilson. "That might be best."

How long did old biddy hair take to style?

"Give me a couple of hours," Cassidy said, reading his mind.

He doubted Mrs. Wilson had enough hair on her head to require two hours of teasing. The former school-teacher flipped off the dryer and began removing her curlers. "I'll take you out to dinner later," he said.

Color flooded Cassidy's cheeks. "You're asking me out on a date?"

A date? He'd already gotten her pregnant, wasn't it a little late for a date? "Uh…" He shook his head. "I was thinking along the lines of a business meeting." He didn't dare become too friendly with Cassidy—she was just too attractive for his peace of mind.

"Oh." The light faded from her eyes and he felt as if he'd kicked a puppy across the barnyard. "Thanks, but I can't leave Mom here by herself."

Recalling the odd way Cassidy's mother had behaved a few minutes ago, he asked, "Is your mother ill?"

"For goodness sake, Logan." Mrs. Wilson formed a capital letter A with her fingers. "Sonja's…"

He stared at the older woman, not having a clue as to what she meant.

"Mom's got Alzheimer's," Cassidy explained.

Alzheimer's? He hadn't heard. Because he'd kept to himself for so long the only person he had any meaningful conversations with was Fletcher. "I'll bring supper here." Logan came up with a mental list of local restaurants and bars. "Tacos sound okay?" Cassidy pressed her fingertips to her mouth and shook her head.

Bethany had suffered morning sickness at all times of the day—that was the only part of pregnancy Logan understood. His wife had always lost the baby before the queasiness abated. He noticed a grill near the tree. "How about steaks on the cooker?"

Cassidy sat up straighter. "Steak sounds good."

With a nod he left. And didn't look back.

As soon as he cleared the trailer park and merged onto the highway to Junket, Logan eased up on the accelerator. Cassidy's face flashed before his eyes. He hadn't meant to hurt her feelings by questioning whether or not the baby was his.

He'd known deep in his gut that he was the father—

but he'd held out hope he wasn't. Cassidy's pregnancy made him feel as if he'd betrayed Bethany's memory. She'd tried for years to have a baby and Cassidy had gotten pregnant during a one-night stand—none of it made sense.

Learning Mrs. Ortiz had Alzheimer's had taken Logan by surprise and confirmed how little he knew about Cassidy's life. Cassidy had been two years behind him in school. He remembered her as a cute, shy girl he'd once helped to collect the contents of her purse after it had spilled in the hallway. He couldn't recall if she'd dated much—he'd been too wrapped up in Bethany to pay attention to other girls.

Cursing, he gripped the wheel tighter. He intended to offer financial assistance with raising the baby but nothing more. He'd figured Cassidy would have plenty of help from family and friends. Now he questioned how she'd manage her hair salon, care for an ailing mother and cope with a new baby.

You could shoulder some of the burden.

Logan's subconscious slammed on the brakes. Cassidy was a sexy, beautiful woman. Spending time with her would sorely test his determination to keep his hands to himself. He blamed his elevated testosterone levels around her on the fact that he hadn't had a normal sex life in years.

Each time Bethany had become pregnant, the bedroom door had closed in his face. She'd been terrified intercourse would cause a miscarriage. As soon as she'd recovered from the inevitable miscarriage he'd been allowed back into the bedroom for stud duty. When Bethany had finally carried a baby through the first trimester, Logan knew he wouldn't have sex again until after the baby had been born. When Cassidy had walked into Billie's Road-house, Logan had been celibate almost a year.

Aside from his celibacy issues, Logan had kept a dirty little secret. Ever since that September night he and Cassidy had ended up in bed together, he'd fantasized about making love to her—most likely because he didn't remember the details of the first time. He'd woken the morning after to her feminine scent on his bed sheets. He'd noticed the towels on the bathroom floor but hadn't remembered taking a shower. A week later he'd discovered a pair of black panties beneath the bed. He'd meant to toss the scrap of lace into the burn barrel—instead he'd stuffed the lingerie in his sock drawer.

After his talk with Cassidy at dinner, Logan intended to keep his distance. He hated to get her hopes up that he'd hang around for the long haul. Cassidy was young and beautiful and sexy. One day she'd find a man who'd marry her despite having a child—Logan's child.

He concentrated on the ribbon of winding road, refusing to contemplate Cassidy falling in love with another man.

Especially when a tiny part of him wanted to be that guy.

"PLEASE WEAR THE YELLOW BLOUSE." Cassidy hovered in the doorway of her mother's bedroom. "Logan will be here any minute for supper." *And my mother is still walking around the house in her bra.*

"I don't want Logan to eat with us."

"An hour ago you were excited about having company. Don't you remember?" Cassidy muttered a curse beneath her breath. Would she ever learn to quit saying *remember?* Sometimes the word upset her mother—other times being reminded of her memory loss didn't faze Sonja.

"Where's my blue shirt? I like the blue shirt." Her mom searched through the nightstand drawer instead of the closet. "Oh, look, Cassidy. Here's my cream." She held up a tube of hand lotion. At the end of every day Cassidy searched the trailer until she found the lotion and returned it to the nightstand.

"You smeared frosting on the blue shirt when you decorated the cookies." *Remember.*

"What cookies?"

Ignoring the question, Cassidy helped her mother slip into the yellow blouse, then grabbed her hand and led her to the recliner in the living room. "Your show is on."

"Oh, good." Her mother pointed the remote at the TV and changed channels every thirty seconds.

Meanwhile Cassidy snuck into the bathroom to brush her teeth, powder her nose and dab a light pink gloss on her lips. She refused to acknowledge how hurt she'd been when Logan had asked if she was certain he had fathered her baby.

The rumble of a truck engine met her ears and she hurried outside. Dusk had descended over the trailer park, and the Millers' Christmas lights blinked on and off, reminding Cassidy again that she needed to decorate before Christmas passed her by.

Out of the corner of her eye she noticed the living-room curtains flutter in Alice and Betty's trailer. Because of her mother's dementia, Cassidy never invited men over. By morning the news of Logan's visit—twice in one day—would have swept through town like a summer wildfire.

Junket was ripe for a new scandal. The last time folks wagged their tongues had been when Fletcher McFadden had filed for divorce from the local banker's daughter after she'd admitted to an affair with a famous bull rider. The *Junket Journal* had carried the story on the front page.

Cassidy was well on her way to becoming Junket's new tabloid tale. Not thirty minutes after Mrs. Wilson left this afternoon, Cassidy's phone had rung off the hook—suddenly everyone needed a trim or color. She'd booked twelve appointments for the following week. At least she had a few days to prepare before she was bombarded with questions.

Is Logan really the father of your baby?

How long have you two been dating?

And questions they didn't dare ask… *Did you have an affair with Logan before Bethany died?*

Are you and Logan getting married?

"Hi," she greeted Logan when he approached the porch.

He set the grocery bag on the step. "Hungry?" The one word sent shivers down her spine. His deep voice reminded her of the husky endearments he'd whispered the night they'd made love.

"Starved."

"If you tell me where the charcoal is, I'll start the grill."

"A bag of briquettes and lighter fluid is beneath the trailer." She pointed to a section of aluminum skirt that housed a storage compartment. "I'll turn on the outdoor lights."

Cassidy grabbed the grocery bag and retreated inside.

She flipped the light switch, then carried the groceries into the kitchen where she noticed the name Bibby's on the bag. Cassidy and her mother never splurged at the local meat market and delicatessen. She traveled into Midland to shop at a discount grocery store chain. The bag contained steaks, twice-baked potatoes and a package of Caesar salad with dressing. She preheated the oven, then cracked open the window to allow fresh air in.

"Are you digging out her Christmas decorations, young man?"

Oh, dear. Cassidy peeked between the blinds and spotted her neighbors standing in their backyard.

"No, ma'am. We're grilling steaks tonight."

"Oh. I'd hoped you might be helping Cassidy string Christmas lights on her trailer," Alice said.

"She's usually the first resident to decorate for the holidays." Betty chimed in. "Her trailer always looks so pretty."

"She didn't—"

"Cassidy has the cutest little Rudolph with a flashing red nose." Alice wiggled her nose and giggled.

"Maybe she's feeling too poorly to fuss over Christmas." Betty crossed her arms over her chest. "With her being in the family way."

The gossip had already been to town and back. If the cousins knew about her pregnancy, so did everyone in the trailer park.

Logan rubbed his neck, which Cassidy guessed was hot enough to ignite without the aid of lighter fluid.

"So Cassidy invited you over for supper?" Alice asked.

"Yes, ma'am."

"Well, it's about time she entertained a man."

Cassidy rolled her eyes. She lived in a trailer, not a bordello.

"Betty, when's the last time Cassidy had a man over?"

"Gosh, I can't remember. A year ago?"

Ugh. Her life was so pathetic.

The bag of briquettes in one hand and lighter fluid in the other, Logan said, "If you'll excuse me, I need to fire up the grill."

"Enjoy your evening. Oh, and Mr. Taylor," Alice said. "If Sonja puts up a fuss send her over here. She likes our fish aquarium."

"Yes, ma'am."

After Logan headed to the other side of the yard, Cassidy closed the window and watched him fuss with the grill. He'd changed clothes since he'd left her place this afternoon. His gray chambray shirt had navy piping across the yoke and pearl snaps up the front. He wore well-worn Wranglers and brown ropers—the quintessential cowboy. And she suspected Logan was a take-charge kind of guy.

Deciding to leave him in peace, Cassidy slipped the potatoes into the oven to warm. Her mother entered the kitchen, stopped in the middle of the room and stared into space, her brain struggling to recall why she stood there.

"What's up, Mom?"

"Oh, hi, honey. When did you get home?"

"A little while ago." *The same fifty or so questions over and over. Day after day. Week after week.* There were times Cassidy wanted to cry. To bawl like a baby. Times she yearned to lash out at her mother…ignore her mother…or leave her mother on someone else's doorstep. Then her mother would smile and say a kind word and Cassidy would feel like the worst daughter in the world for her uncharitable thoughts. "Would you set the table for three?"

Her mother retrieved the plates, then gasped. "That man is setting our tree on fire."

Flames shot sky high from the small grill. It was a miracle the cooker hadn't melted. She poked her head out the door. "The hose is on the other side of the trailer."

Logan almost smiled and the gesture tugged at her heart. "Got carried away with the lighter fluid." Then he asked, "Steaks ready?"

Ready? Oops, she'd forgotten to season them. She shut the door and tore the butcher paper from the meat, then muttered out loud, "Where's the garlic salt?"

"Juan loved garlic."

Juan was Cassidy's father.

Alzheimer's hadn't tarnished her mother's memory of Juan—a man Cassidy had never met. Some days her mother would go on forever about the love of her youth. Cassidy couldn't care less about her father. She searched the cupboard, found steak seasoning and sprinkled the spice over the meat. Grabbing a pair of tongs, she said, "Be right back."

"Here." She offered the plate to Logan. A rich, spicy scent—his cologne—competed with the smell of lighter fluid lingering in the air.

His fingers slid over her hand when he took the plate and she had to force herself to release the dish as memories of those same hands caressing her breasts…her thighs…her…"Nice of you to bring a steak for Mom," she said, slamming the door on the x-rated thoughts.

He shrugged off her gratitude.

Cassidy sensed Logan was a nice, decent man. For the baby's sake she was glad.

"Mom makes people uncomfortable. I hope she doesn't offend you tonight."

"How long has she been this way?" he asked.

Sonja Ortiz's health had begun deteriorating after Cassidy graduated from high school. "For a while. The last two years have been especially trying. Eventually I'll have to put her in a home."

"I'm sorry." Compassion shone in his brown eyes.

"Now more than ever I wish my mother wasn't ill." Cassidy glanced over her shoulder at the trailer. "She'd have been thrilled to pieces to be a grandmother."

"About the baby…"

She should have kept her mouth shut—at least until they'd eaten.

"I'm more than willing, in fact, I insist on helping you out financially. But—"

Her breath caught in her lungs. The stark pain in his gaze proved how much the news of her pregnancy had shaken him. An overwhelming sense of sadness filled her. "You don't want to raise this child."

"No."

Compassion battled anger. She'd never been in Logan's shoes. Never loved someone and then had that love ripped from her arms the way his wife and their baby had been taken from him.

"We'll be fine on our own, Logan." The words sounded bold and brave but Cassidy's insides shook. How on earth would she handle caring for an infant, cutting hair every day and watching over her mother? *Mom managed and you will, too.* "I told you about the baby because you had a right to know." She searched his expression but his face remained composed, no hint that her words affected him one way or the other. "The potatoes will be done in ten minutes." She left the brooding cowboy in peace.

Ten minutes later—not a second sooner—Logan rapped on the door and stepped into the kitchen. He set the steaks on the counter.

"What would you prefer to drink?" she asked. "We have red wine." Her mother's favorite. "Or soda or bottled water."

"Water's fine."

"Have a seat." She placed the drinks on the table. "Time for supper, Mom." Cassidy cut her mother's steak into bite-size pieces and poured dressing on the salad, aware of Logan's eyes following her movements.

Cassidy dug into her potato as she stewed over Logan's announcement that he wouldn't be involved in their baby's life. Yes, her mother had raised her without a father and she was a well-adjusted young woman— in her opinion. But she wanted better than that for her child. She wanted her little boy or girl to know the love of a mother and a father.

When Logan still hadn't touched his food, she asked, "What's wrong?"

"Shouldn't we wait for your mother?"

"I gave up forcing her to come to the table. She'll eat when she's ready."

Logan picked at his meal, ruining Cassidy's appetite. She set her fork and knife aside. "I get not wanting anything to do with me, Logan. I'm a big girl. I know there weren't any feelings involved in what we…did."

She cleared her throat and continued. "But I don't understand how you can walk away from your own child."

"I'm not walking away. I said I would help financially."

Tired and frustrated, she lashed out. "How do you plan to ignore a child who'll grow up right under your nose?" She had no plans to leave Junket. This was home.

He shoved his chair away from the table and headed for the door.

Great. She'd pushed him too far. "So that's it? You'll send a check in the mail once a month?"

Hand on the doorknob, he said. "That's all I have to offer."

There went all her pie-in-the-sky dreams of her child having a real family. "You know what, Logan? Never mind. Never mind the money. Never mind me. Never mind the baby. We don't need your help."

The muscle along his jaw pulsed in anger. After a moment, he opened the door and walked out, leaving Cassidy the last word.

And the last regret.

Chapter Three

"What am I going to do about her, Twister?"

Her meaning Cassidy.

His deaf companion chased his tail, ignoring the cattle grazing nearby. "No comment, eh?" Logan sat astride his horse staring at the sea of yellow grass ending at the horizon. He clicked his tongue. The horse moved forward and Twister raced off in a different direction.

Logan had been checking for breaks in the fence line since dawn—three hours ago. The flat-for-as-far-as-the-eye-could-see terrain and a lonely wind whistling in his ears created perfect contemplating conditions. And contemplate he did.

Three days had passed since Cassidy Ortiz had dropped the bomb that he was about to become a father. Logan had yet to wrap his brain around the news. He hadn't meant to hurt Cassidy when he'd confessed he had no intention of becoming involved in their child's life, but her shocked expression said he'd failed miserably.

Spotting a broken wire, Logan stopped the horse and retrieved the tools tied to the saddle. A few months ago he'd considered replacing this section of fence, which ran along the western border of the ranch, but he'd gotten sidetracked nursing a sick cow. Now he didn't dare waste money on new barbed wire when he'd soon have to fork over a monthly child-support check.

Cassidy said to never mind about the money—remember?

Ignoring the voice in his head playing devil's advocate, Logan used the fence stretcher to pull the two broken ends of barbed wire taut, then fed the lines into a Gripple. The small metal cylinder prevented the wires from slipping back out. Satisfied with his handiwork, he rode on.

Cassidy hadn't asked for a handout but the income from her hair salon wouldn't cover the added expenses associated with raising a kid—diapers, baby formula, clothes, toys, doctor visits…college. Things he and Bethany had discussed, anticipated, then tried to forget with each failed pregnancy. Bethany's and his baby's deaths had gutted Logan. The only thing he had left to give was his money.

Tell Cassidy why you can't be the child's father.

After Bethany's death he'd written off marriage and children for good. He'd had his chance at family and he'd blown it. Not even Pastor Ferguson had been able to convince Logan that Bethany and the baby were in a better place. How was dead better?

Cassidy has no one to turn to.

Although Logan's intention had been to spare himself more emotional grief by staying on the fringes, deep in his gut he admitted he couldn't stand by and not lift a finger to help.

For months he had hardened himself from the inside out—insulating his heart and soul against the pleasures of life. Not until he'd sat down at the kitchen table in Cassidy's trailer had he realized the depth of his loneliness. The warmth of her home had wrapped around his cold heart and squeezed. Despite his reservations he'd do his best to be there for Cassidy and the baby.

"Looks like we're done here, Twister." An hour later both horse and dog had been fed, watered and settled in the barn. Twister preferred sleeping outside year-round and Logan had made up a bed of hay for the animal in one of the empty horse stalls.

There were a hundred chores that needed doing, but he hadn't been able to shake the restless feeling plaguing him since supper at Cassidy's trailer. *Screw the chores.* He showered and changed clothes, then grabbed the truck keys and headed into town.

With a population under three hundred the town wasn't much more than a map dot. One four-way stop. Two historical buildings—the feed store, which had been around since 1864, and the bank, circa 1923. Baker's Drugstore, now owned by the Polanskis managed to stay in business, but Maria's Cantina had gone under. Two bars—Davies on the corner and the Tap House across the street from the bank were the local watering holes. A lone barbershop. Crusty's Pizza. There were two blocks of residential homes but many of the locals who didn't ranch lived in the same trailer park as Cassidy on the outskirts of town and worked at the fertilizer factory located between Junket and Midland.

The town council had voted on new Christmas decorations last year and Logan noticed the wreaths that now hung from the lamp posts along the sidewalk. The posts themselves had been wrapped with white lights and large red pots filled with poinsettias sat on the corners of both sides of the street.

He parked in front of the drugstore and went inside. The cow bell attached to the door handle announced his presence. He heard female voices and recognized one of them as the store owner's—Helga Polanski. He headed for the beauty department where Helga stocked the men's razor blades and shaving cream. As he searched for his brand, the women's voices grew louder.

"I can't believe Cassidy Ortiz is pregnant."

"Well now, it's best not to jump to conclusions," Helga said.

"Mabel Wilson claims Logan asked Cassidy if the baby was his."

Logan's ears burned.

"What did she say?" Helga asked.

"Mabel said Cassidy got to feelin' poorly and had to sit down before she gave him an answer."

"See there. We don't know for sure whose baby it is."

"Logan's had a rough time."

Logan believed the second voice belonged to Mrs. Gilbert, the local school-board president. The woman had a nasty habit of butting into people's private affairs. "That poor man drags himself around town like a beaten dog."

Jeez, did he look that pathetic?

"I bet Cassidy's hoping to trap Logan into marrying her." Mrs. Gilbert lowered her voice and Logan edged toward the end of the aisle. "You know Cassidy's mother had her out of wedlock."

If he didn't acknowledge that he was the father of Cassidy's baby folks would believe the worst of her.

"Sonja did just fine raising Cassidy on her own," Helga said.

"I wouldn't doubt she's looking for a handout."

Handout? Logan recalled Cassidy's face as she told him she didn't need his help.

"If Cassidy's pregnant she'll expect our understanding not our censure." At least Helga possessed a little compassion.

"I don't know how that girl manages. Wilma stopped by for tea this morning and said Cassidy had to drive Sonja into Midland for another doctor's appointment today."

"Cassidy takes good care of her mother. Can't find fault with her for that."

Logan had heard enough. Cassidy didn't deserve to be talked about. "Afternoon, ladies." He walked up the aisle.

Helga's face flushed beet-red and Mrs. Gilbert's mouth sagged open—wide enough to see the silver fillings in her bottom molars.

"What brings you by this afternoon, Logan?" Helga smoothed a hand down the front of the white smock she wore over her long-sleeved blouse.

He lifted the shaving supplies in his hand.

"I'd better go." The school-board president flashed a nervous smile.

"Before you leave, Mrs. Gilbert, I'd like to set the record straight." The old biddy's eyes rounded. "The rumors are true. I'm the father of Cassidy's baby." He glanced at both women. "You'll see that the correct information makes the rounds, won't you?"

Mrs. Gilbert nodded, then scurried off.

Helga wrung her hands. "That was rude of us. I'm sorry for gossiping."

Ignoring the apology, he asked, "Where can I find a blow-up snowman like the one next to the checkout counter up front?"

"We've got several in the storeroom."

If Logan intended to change Cassidy's we-don't-need-your-help attitude, he'd best do so bearing gifts.

WHAT IN THE WORLD?

Cassidy parked the car and gaped at her trailer—lit up like a cheap motel off the Las Vegas strip.

"Look, Cassidy. Isn't that pretty?" Her mother leaned forward and stared out the windshield.

Strands of colored lights outlined the trailer, its windows and the door. More lights had been wound around the porch rails, down the steps and stretched along the short sidewalk like an airport runway. And icicle lights hung from the gutters. She hadn't remembered buying those last year, but maybe she had.

The large red and white peppermint lollipops she'd purchased during the after-Christmas sales were stuck in the ground along the edge of the grass and white lights had been wrapped around the sticks. Rudolph stood in the middle of the yard with his blinking red nose. Every few seconds he turned his head and pawed the ground. Her Christmas wreath made of miniature Santa Clauses hung on the door and one made of wrapped gift boxes decorated the front window.

The carport next door was empty. As soon as her neighbors arrived home she'd thank them. Betty and Alice must have dug out the Christmas boxes from underneath the trailer right after Cassidy had left to take her mother to the doctor's earlier in the day.

Cassidy got out of the car, then froze when her gaze swept the side yard. Forgetting her mother for the moment, she stared at the glittering display. White lights circled the trunk of the cherry tree. Lighted blue balls the size of cantaloupes hung from the lower branches—another bargain from last year. Cassidy's hair-cutting shed sported more icicle lights and—*whoa, where had that come from?* A life-size inflatable snowman with a plastic scarf fluttering around its neck stood next to the back door.

Pure happiness filled Cassidy and she laughed with joy. The snowman was gaudy and big and she loved it. Christmas was her favorite holiday, but this year she struggled with the blues because of her pregnancy. She wanted the baby—that had never been the issue. But the circumstances surrounding her pregnancy had dampened her usual excitement for the holiday. She owed her neighbors a big hug for putting the *Merry* back into her Christmas.

An hour later her mother was settled in bed with a stack of magazines, which she'd read until she fell asleep. Cassidy slipped on a sweater and sat on the porch steps, watching the twinkling blue balls twirl in the breeze. The doctor appointment hadn't gone well. Her mother had enough wits left about her to realize Dr. Klinger had been testing her memory. When he'd asked Sonja's opinion of the new president, she said, "What do *you* think of the new president?"

When asked the day of the week…

"I'm retired. Every day is Saturday."

In the end the verdict had been the same—medication wasn't slowing the progression of the disease. Her mother's memory continued to deteriorate.

Eyes welling with tears, Cassidy rested her hand against her stomach. She'd hoped for better news. Not only did she not have her mother to lean on during this pregnancy but her mother would never know her grandchild in the traditional sense. Dr. Klinger had warned Cassidy that Sonja might feel threatened by the baby and become more cantankerous.

When they'd left the office, the doctor had given Cassidy information on convalescent homes specializing in the care of Alzheimer's patients. Her mother's retirement fund would cover three years at the most, then she'd have to transfer to a facility subsidized by Medicare and forfeit her social security check.

Logan said he'd help.

With the baby, not her mother.

An image of Logan filled her mind. The man was a looker. If they had a son, he'd grow up to be tall and strong like Logan. A daughter would be the perfect height—somewhere between Cassidy's five-feet five and Logan's six-foot whatever. Whether girl or boy they'd have brown eyes and dark hair.

The other night Cassidy's heart had ached at the despair in Logan's eyes when he'd insisted he wanted nothing to do with raising their child. Instead of her pregnancy making Logan happy, she suspected her condition simply brought up sad memories for him.

The cowboy had made it clear he wouldn't be pushed into doing anything he didn't want to do—well, neither would she. She'd meant what she'd said—she didn't need Logan. Her mother had managed without a man. Raised Cassidy without the help of a husband or grandparents. Cassidy would do the same for her child.

The sound of crunching gravel caught her attention. Betty and Alice had arrived home. She walked to the front yard where she found the women admiring the trailer. "I can't thank you enough for doing such an incredible job decorating."

"We didn't string the lights." Betty peeked at the side yard. "Alice, come see this."

The ladies *ooh'd* and *ahh'd*.

Bewildered, Cassidy trailed after the women. "You didn't buy the snowman?"

They shook their heads.

Then who? She supposed any of her neighbors might have fixed up the yard since they all knew where she stored the decorations. "Maybe the Millers felt bad that they beat me to the punch."

The older women smiled.

"What?" Cassidy asked.

Alice giggled. "I think we know who did this."

"Who?"

"That nice young man you invited over for supper a few nights ago." Betty winked, then nodded to Cassidy's stomach and whispered, "The baby's father."

"Logan?" *No.* Logan wouldn't do this. Not after she'd insisted she didn't want his help.

If it was Logan… *Why?* Had he changed his mind about being involved in her and the baby's life? Or was this *favor* done out of guilt because he intended to keep his distance?

"How did the doctor visit go?" Betty asked.

"He said I should consider putting Mom in a home sooner rather than later."

"For heaven's sake. Sonja's not that bad. She hasn't

started the trailer on fire." Betty quirked a pencil-thin eyebrow. "Has she?"

"No, but the doctor warned that Mom might become jealous and hurt the baby."

"We'll help, dear," Alice said. "We'll watch the baby while you cut hair."

"Or," Betty added. "We'll keep Sonja occupied when you need time alone with the baby."

Tears stung Cassidy's eyes. The women's generosity humbled her. "Thank you. I'd like to keep Mom with me as long as possible."

"When is your due date?" Alice asked.

"Early June. I'm scheduled for an ultrasound on Friday. I'll know for sure after that."

"We'll sit with Sonja while you go to the appointment," Betty said.

"I'd planned to bring Mom with me."

"No, no, dear. That's a special time for you and the baby's father."

Her and Logan? Cassidy hadn't thought to tell Logan about the ultrasound.

Betty cleared her throat. "He is going with you, isn't he?"

"Of course." She crossed her fingers inside the pocket of her sweater. She didn't have the energy to explain her relationship with Logan—whatever it was—to her neighbors. "I'm getting chilled. I think I'll go inside."

The women murmured good-night and walked off.

Tomorrow Cassidy would drive out to Logan's ranch and thank him for the snowman and for hanging her Christmas lights. Depending on her reception she might even mention the ultrasound.

LOGAN HAD JUST STEPPED OUT of the shower when Twister's bark alerted him that he had company. *Probably Fletcher.* Needing advice on how to handle the situation with Cassidy, Logan had left a message on his friend's cell to stop by when he had a minute.

In truth, he was surprised Fletcher hadn't phoned as soon as he'd heard the gossip that Logan had fathered Cassidy's baby. Then again his buddy might have been too busy with his new online love interest to pay attention to the latest hearsay.

After toweling dry he slipped on jeans and socks, then shoved his feet into his boots. He hurried into the bedroom and grabbed a clean shirt from the closet. Thrusting his arms through the sleeves he hustled downstairs. "'Bout time you showed your ugly—" he opened the door "—Cassidy."

She stood on the front porch, a tentative smile lighting her face. Then her gaze shifted to his chest—his naked chest. He heard a tiny gasp of air escape her mouth. Logan swallowed a groan. No sense denying they were attracted to each other—the two feet of space separating them sizzled. All Cassidy had to do was breathe and Logan's hormones went haywire.

"I came at a bad time." The statement left her mouth in a husky murmur, the sound familiar to the whiskey-laced voice he heard in his dreams. His attention shifted from her mouth to the baby-blue sweater hugging her breasts—breasts he'd already seen, touched and kissed—but damned if he could remember.

"Sorry." He fumbled with his shirt snaps. "I mucked

out horse stalls this morning and…" He sounded like a bumbling idiot.

"May I come in?"

"Yeah, sure." He stepped aside and she slipped past him, the scent of her shampoo teasing his nose. Today she wore her hair in a ponytail, making her appear almost too young to be having a baby. *His baby.*

Her gaze roamed the entryway, zeroing in on the dust bunnies in the corners. Aside from washing the bed sheets once a week and cleaning the bathroom and kitchen, the house had remained untouched since his wife's death. He supposed if Cassidy intended to visit on occasion he ought to run the vacuum more than once every six months.

"Can I get you something to drink?" he asked.

She shook her head. "I stopped by to thank you." Her brown eyes glowed. "I'm guessing you strung the Christmas lights around my trailer."

Ignoring the slow and steady rush of warmth spreading through his chest he said, "The other night the women next door to you mentioned that you hadn't had time to decorate." He had no idea why he'd gone overboard except that he'd wanted to make up for acting like an ass. "And you shouldn't hang lights in your condition. You don't want to take the chance of falling and hurting the baby."

The glow in her eyes cooled and her mouth drew into a thin line. *What the heck?* Why would his concern about her pregnancy upset her? Isn't that what she wanted from him—to care about the baby?

"You shouldn't have bought the snowman," she said.

The blow-up monstrosity was as tacky as the other decorations in her yard. "You don't like it?"

Her gaze shifted to the wall clock. "I like the snowman, but it must have been expensive."

Did guilt come with a price tag? He'd purchased the snowman to appease his guilt—guilt that by all rights he shouldn't feel, but did. Shoot, he hadn't invited Cassidy to Billie's Roadhouse. Hadn't begged her for a lift. Hadn't invited her inside the house.

Logan hadn't asked for any of this.

Neither had Cassidy.

"You shouldn't have driven out here." Her eyes widened. "I mean shouldn't you be home resting?" Cassidy had to take care of an ailing mother, then stand on her feet all day and cut hair. That couldn't be good for her or the baby.

"I'm fine." She flung her ponytail over her shoulder. "Besides thanking you for decorating my trailer I wanted—" She cleared her throat. "Tomorrow I'm having an ultrasound done at my doctor's appointment."

The oxygen in his lungs crystallized and burned the lining.

"Maybe you'd like to come along and see a picture of the baby."

The pain increased until his insides felt on fire. He didn't want to go. Didn't want to be reminded of the afternoon he and Bethany had discovered they were having a baby girl. But the idea of Cassidy driving into Midland by herself—taking the same highway Bethany had taken the day she…

"What time do I need to pick you up?"

Chapter Four

The next afternoon, surrounded by a sea of big bellies and fussing toddlers, Cassidy and Logan sat in the waiting room of the doctor's office in Midland.

She snuck a peek at Logan and cringed. Eyes wide, mouth pinched, the man might as well have had the words *shoot me* stamped on his forehead in capital letters. She swallowed a sigh. She wasn't upset with Logan. She was miffed at herself for being insensitive. Until this moment she hadn't considered today's outing might dredge up bad memories.

Last week when Logan had announced he'd wanted nothing to do with raising their child, she'd been convinced he still grieved for Bethany and their unborn baby. But when he'd given her the giant blow-up snowman and strung Christmas lights around her trailer, she'd wondered if there might be a chance—a tiny chance—that he'd make room in his heart for her and their baby. Then he'd confessed he'd helped her because he'd been afraid she might injure herself or the baby.

"If you'd rather wait downstairs in the lobby, I understand." And she did. As a matter of fact she'd prefer Logan leave, so she'd stop feeling guilty.

His blank stare prompted a second try. "You look as if you need fresh air."

Logan set aside the magazine he'd opened but hadn't read.

"Cassidy Ortiz," a nurse called.

Would he leave or stay? She didn't wait to find out. Zigzagging between the toddlers playing on the carpet, Cassidy smiled as she approached the nurse.

The RN's attention fixated on Logan who stood by his chair, his gaze darting between Cassidy and the EXIT.

"He's not—" Cassidy's sentence trailed off when Logan crossed the room—somber, like a man heading to the gallows. The pregnant moms ogled him, mistakenly assuming the father-to-be was nervous.

Leaving the nurse to wait for Logan, Cassidy walked to the weight scale at the end of the hall. She knew the drill. After slipping off her clogs, she stepped on the platform. Logan stopped a discreet distance away, allowing her a modicum of privacy.

"How are you feeling?" The nurse slid the bar upward along the balance beam.

"Fine." In truth Cassidy felt pudgy and her legs and lower back ached after styling hair all day.

"You're a little underweight."

So much for privacy. The announcement brought a frown to Logan's face. Ignoring his glower, Cassidy entered the exam room.

"Clothes off from the waist down." The nurse handed Cassidy a paper sheet. "Dr. Gilda will be with you in a moment." The door closed, almost smacking Logan in the face when he turned to follow.

He grappled for the doorknob. "I'll wait outside." Then he vanished.

Relieved, she removed her clothes, hopped onto the exam table and arranged the paper sheet over the lower half of her body. She neglected to call out that the coast was clear, assuming Logan had fled.

"Look what I found in the hallway." Dr. Gilda swept into the room, a pale-faced Logan trailing her.

His gaze clashed with Cassidy's and the stark pain darkening his brown eyes pierced her heart. He didn't want to be here, yet he hadn't abandoned her.

"Your blood workup looks fine," the doctor said, reading Cassidy's chart. "I'm worried about your weight. Morning sickness still bothering you?"

"Certain foods make me queasy."

"Try increasing your in-between-meal snacks." Dr. Gilda set Cassidy's medical chart aside. "Let's do the ultrasound first, then I'll examine you."

"Will we be able to get an exact due date?" Cassidy reclined on the table.

"We should." The doctor slid the machine closer, then lowered the sheet, exposing Cassidy's slightly rounded tummy.

Dr. Gilda smiled at Logan. "Dad, you're welcome to hold mom's hand while I point to things on the monitor."

Logan inched closer, but not close enough to touch her.

The doctor squeezed the clear jelly on her stomach and spread it around with the transducer probe. "Were you wanting to know the sex of the baby?"

"Yes." Cassidy spoke.

"No," Logan said at the same time.

Dr. Gilda moved the probe across Cassidy's belly.

If not for the panic swirling in Logan's brown eyes she might have ignored his silent plea. "I guess the father wants to be surprised," she said around the lump in her throat.

"The baby's developing fine." The doctor pressed several buttons and two printed photos emerged. "Your due date is June twelfth." The doctor wiped the gel off Cassidy's stomach. "Let's do a quick internal exam—"

"I'll wait outside." The door shut before Logan's announcement had registered with Cassidy.

"Everything all right between you and the father?" Dr. Gilda asked.

No. "The baby was a surprise." *A whopper of a surprise.* "I'd like to know the baby's sex."

"It's a boy." The doctor handed one of the ultrasound pictures to Cassidy, then pointed to a spot on the film. "There's the proof."

Cassidy's heart melted. She'd hoped for a boy. What man could resist having a son to throw the football to or to go fishing with?

"Everything's fine, Cassidy." The doctor helped her sit up. "Any questions or concerns?"

Now that Logan wasn't in the room… "A few days ago I had a little spotting. Nothing much."

"Spotting isn't unusual but I want you to take it easy. Stay off your feet as much as possible. Let's see you in a week or so—Tuesday the twenty-second."

"That soon?"

"This is your first baby. Nothing wrong in being cautious."

"But that's two days before Christmas." Betty and Alice had plans to travel to Galveston to visit friends that week and Cassidy had no one to watch her mother.

"Are you spending the holidays somewhere else?" the doctor asked.

"No. I'll be here."

The doctor paused at the door and smiled. "Have a good day."

Cassidy dressed, then stepped into the hallway. No Logan. Same in the waiting room—no Logan. After scheduling her next appointment, she used the restroom, then rode the elevator to the lobby.

Logan.

He stood in front of the floor-to-ceiling windows, watching traffic whiz by on the street outside. She wished she knew him better but in reality they were nothing more than acquaintances. They'd lived in the same town all their lives but had said little more than "Hi" and "Hello" a handful of times.

And then we made a baby together.

Her heart insisted Logan was a nice guy and wanted to do right by her and the baby—as best his broken heart would allow. Cassidy wasn't sure that would be enough.

She stopped next to him and studied his profile. A muscle ticked along his jaw and squint lines fanned from the corner of his eye—as if he hadn't opened his eyes all the way since his wife's death. Less painful to view the world in slivers of light than through a wide-open lens.

Cassidy wouldn't have invited Logan along today and caused him such turmoil if not for that darned blow-up snowman. She'd convinced herself his gift had been a cry for attention—that Logan needed a reason to start living again—Cassidy yearned to be that reason.

Oh, grow up. She wasn't a princess and Logan was no knight in shining armor riding to her rescue. Cassidy knew the difference between real life and fairy tales, but that didn't prevent her from dreaming of Logan giving more of himself to her and their son than just his time or money.

She cleared her throat and his gaze settled on her reflection in the window. Not even the dark film protecting the glass disguised his desolate expression. Without a word, he held open the lobby door for her, then escorted her across the parking lot. Cassidy gripped his warm callused hand longer than necessary when he helped her into the truck.

"Would you like to grab a bite to eat?" he asked.

Her heart skipped a beat until she remembered Dr. Gilda's warning that she needed to gain weight. She suspected Logan's invitation had more to do with her health than wanting to be with her. "Sure."

Logan shut the truck door, then hopped in on the driver's side. "What's your preference?"

"I haven't had good barbecue in ages."

A hint of a smile teased the corner of his mouth. "I know a great place." As he pulled out of the parking lot she decided right then and there she'd coax a real smile out of Logan by the end of the day.

"WELCOME TO HOG HEAVEN," a waitress named Arianna greeted Logan and Cassidy when they entered the restaurant on the outskirts of Midland.

"Table for two." Logan ignored the way the girl's

gaze rolled over him. In another lifetime he might have been flattered, but he was too emotionally drained to care if a female found him appealing.

Liar. You care what Cassidy thinks of you.

In truth his male ego did appreciate Cassidy's physical attraction to him, although he didn't dare delve too deeply into the reasons why. He was better off not contemplating anything that involved emotions or feelings.

Arianna popped her gum. "Follow me."

Halfway to their booth Logan noticed his fingers rested against the small of Cassidy's back. The fresh scent of her shampoo and the delicate curve of her spine reminded him how much he missed the little intimacies between a man and a woman—fleeting touches and secret smiles.

He waited for Cassidy to pick her seat, then slid in across from her. The waitress took their drink orders—Cassidy requested water. Logan chose a Coke.

"I'll drive home if you want a beer," Cassidy said.

Did he look like he needed a beer?

"Yes." Her dark eyes sparkled.

"Yes, what?"

"You look like you need a beer."

Her smile tugged a grin from him. "Are you a mind reader?"

"I've had plenty of practice with Mom. More often than not I have to guess what she's thinking, because she can't remember." Cassidy traced her fingertip over a scratch in the surface of the table. "I'm sorry, Logan."

He hated apologies—mostly because he sucked at them. "For what?"

"Pressuring you into going with me today."

"I could have said no." He lied. Allowing Cassidy to go alone hadn't been an option.

"I'm usually not insensitive to people's feelings." She placed her hand on top of his. "I imagine the doctor's office triggered bad memories."

If Cassidy knew the real reason he'd fled to the lobby she'd push harder to insinuate herself into his life. He hadn't been thinking of Bethany in the exam room. He'd wanted to learn the baby's sex so damned bad but had feared the knowledge would chip away at his resolve to keep his emotional distance from Cassidy and the baby.

As soon as they'd entered the restaurant, Logan had chastised himself for suggesting the outing. He didn't wish to make a habit of eating with Cassidy. This time he had an excuse—she needed to gain weight. But what about next time? Was he nuts to believe he could go it alone for the rest of his life?

The waitress delivered the drinks. "Ready to order?"

They hadn't even studied the menus. "We need a few more minutes," he said.

"Take your time." Arianna winked as she waltzed off.

"How did Bethany handle that?"

"Handle what?"

"Women ogling you."

"Women don't ogle me." He opened the menu and pretended to view the choices, though he already knew what he'd order.

"Bethany said once that she never understood why you settled for her when every girl in school wanted to date you." Cassidy set her menu aside. "I told her you picked her because you loved her."

Throat tight, Logan chugged his Coke. He had loved Bethany. She was his first love. And he'd never strayed—not even when his wife's miscarriages had put a strain on their marriage. "Bethany's the one who could have done better."

He'd married his high school sweetheart believing they'd be together forever. He'd never expected them to have trouble starting a family. Years of stress, depression and too many trips to the E.R. in the middle of the night had taken a toll on their relationship. Logan regretted that their marriage hadn't been stronger…happier at the time of Bethany's death. Enough of the past. "Betty and Alice are nice ladies."

"They're helpful neighbors and Mom enjoys their company."

Relieved Cassidy played along with the change in topic, he asked, "How long will you be able to keep your mother with you?"

"Not as long as I'd hoped. Her condition is deteriorating rapidly. That happens when a person's diagnosed at a young age. Mom's only forty-seven." Tears welled in Cassidy's eyes. "Once or twice a day she has a clear thought and for a split second she's the mom I remember. The mom who worked overtime at the fertilizer factory to save up for a down payment on the trailer. The mom who encouraged me to go to beauty school instead of working alongside her at the factory."

"I'm sorry." He wished he could fix Sonja's memory for Cassidy.

She waved her hand. "Hopefully Mom's not giving Alice and Betty a difficult time this afternoon."

"We can get our orders to go, if you'd rather—"

"No, I'm enjoying the break." She winced. "That sounded bad, didn't it?"

Logan was no authority on patience. "No brothers or sisters to help with your mother?" he asked.

"I'm an only child. My father and mother never married."

"Do you keep in touch your father?"

"No. He's never been a part of my life." She shrugged. "To tell you the truth, I don't care."

Cassidy cared—the catch in her voice betrayed her. Cassidy's father had abandoned her. Logan wanted to argue that paying child support was taking responsibility for their baby but in truth he was no better than her father. Logan hadn't considered how the child would feel when they learned their father had chosen not to be involved in their life. Would his daughter or son grow up to despise him?

Was it possible to be a part of the baby's life without committing his heart?

"Ready?" Arianna stopped by the table, order pad in hand.

"I'll have the sweet and sour barbecued ribs," Cassidy said.

"And for you?" Arianna winked at Logan.

"The barbecue chicken sandwich."

"Side orders of fries and cold slaw?" Arianna glanced between them.

"That's fine," Cassidy answered.

"I'll fetch ya'll refills." The waitress grabbed the menus and sauntered off.

After a stilted silence, Cassidy asked, "How's the cattle business?"

"I've decreased the size of the herd." Because he hadn't wanted any extra cowboys hanging out at the ranch watching him mope.

Cattle talk exhausted, Cassidy tapped her fingers to the music playing on the jukebox. After a few minutes Arianna appeared with their meals and drinks. "Anything else?"

"No, this looks great." Cassidy stuffed a paper napkin inside the collar of her shirt. Then she dug out a clip from her purse and secured the long strands of her hair to the top of her head. "What's wrong?" she asked Logan.

"Nothing." *Just that your hair looks sexy like that.* He waited for her to sample the ribs.

"Wow." Another bite. "Mmm." Sauce dotted the corners of her mouth. "Here." She offered a rib from her plate. "Try one."

Amused by her enthusiasm he chuckled, the sound rattling his rusty pipes. "I've had them before." Cassidy's obvious enjoyment pleased him and any regrets about suggesting the meal vanished.

She flashed a barbecue-stained smile.

"What?"

"You're grinning," she said.

"And you've got sauce all over your face." He dipped the corner of his napkin into her water glass, then rubbed her skin, his eyes glued to her lips. A surge of desire caught him square in the gut. He wanted to taste her mouth. Right here. Right now.

"Is something wrong, Logan?"

Her voice startled him. "Nothing." He dropped the napkin on the table and dug into his sandwich.

When Cassidy finished half her meal, he asked, "Aside from needing to gain more weight, did the doctor give you and the baby a clean bill of health?"

"We're both fine. I have another appointment the Tuesday before Christmas."

"That soon?"

"Routine lab work."

Logan wanted to ask why she needed more lab work done, but kept his mouth shut. The less he knew the easier to keep from caring too much.

"What are your plans for Christmas?" *Oh, hell.* She'd assume he was angling for an invitation to spend the day with her.

Aren't you?

No. Maybe. A few weeks ago he hadn't planned to celebrate the holiday. After making a trip to the cemetery to put flowers on Bethany and his father's graves, he'd intended to sit in the house and watch TV all day. Now he wasn't sure he wanted to be alone.

"Mom and I open gifts in the morning, then watch movies all day." She wiped her fingers on a napkin. "Are you planning to visit your mother?"

"No. She and my aunt are traveling to the Florida Keys with a senior citizens' group." His mother had moved to Florida to be closer to her sister after Logan's father passed away. She'd offered to drive to Junket this year, but he'd been determined to spend his first Christmas without Bethany alone.

"You're welcome to come over. I'm fixing a roast and all the trimmings for supper."

He opened his mouth to say *no thanks* but the words vanished.

Cassidy rubbed her stomach. "I'm full."

"No room for dessert?" he asked.

She shook her head, her attention on the two couples who'd walked onto the dance floor. A George Strait song played on the jukebox. "I haven't danced in forever."

Dance with her. She hasn't asked for a damned thing from you. The least you could do is twirl her around the floor. Tired of fighting the need to keep his distance from her both physically and emotionally, he slid from the booth and held out his hand.

Her mouth curved upward as she placed her hand in his and he led her to the dance floor.

Her sweet scent surrounded him and her messy hair rubbed his face. He pulled her close…closer…there. With her hips nestled against his groin, her breasts pressed into his chest and her head snuggled beneath his chin, he closed his eyes and absorbed the feeling of peace spreading through him.

It's just a hug.

Hell, they both needed a hug. The song's lyrics faded into the background until all he heard and felt was Cassidy humming to the music and their bodies rubbing against each other.

One song faded into another and another. Then Cassidy gazed into his eyes. *Kiss her.* Unable to stop himself he lowered his head an inch at a time.

Right or wrong he needed this kiss. Her sigh of surrender when his lips touched hers filled his soul. She tasted of tangy barbecue and a sweetness all her own. The warmth spreading through Logan's chest had nothing to do with the hardness growing between his thighs.

Her arms tightened around his neck and he surrendered to her embrace.

Cassidy was his haven. His refuge.

Cassidy was trouble with a capital T.

Chapter Five

At eleven-thirty on Saturday Cassidy took her first break of the morning. The two weeks leading up to Christmas were among the busiest of the year. She cut, curled, bleached and colored hair from sunup to sundown. After making her mother a sandwich, Cassidy microwaved the take-out order of ribs that Logan had insisted on buying for her yesterday before they'd left Hog Heaven. She closed her eyes and savored the tangy barbecue flavor while the George Strait tune she and Logan had danced to played over and over in her mind.

Recalling how tenderly Logan had held her in his arms and how intimate their kiss had been made her yearn to believe his feelings for her were deepening, but she suspected his concern was born from a sense of responsibility toward her and the baby. A baby he supposedly wanted nothing to do with.

She'd meant what she'd said the day she'd advised him of her pregnancy—she and the baby didn't need him. She was nothing if not her mother's daughter. Cassidy wasn't afraid to take care of herself or support the baby—but had she spoken too hastily?

All these years she and her mother had survived without Cassidy's father. How different their lives might have been had her father hung around. A child deserved two parents. She had to make Logan see that their son needed more than a support check—he needed a father's attention. Love. Guidance.

And what about you, Cassidy? What do you need from Logan?

Her feelings for Logan were a jumbled mess. She cared about him—what woman in her right mind wouldn't be sympathetic toward a man who'd lost his wife and child? The fact that he refused to move on with his life angered Cassidy.

That's because you're falling in love with him.

Thinking about Logan frustrated her so she focused on eating, then cleaned up the kitchen and returned to the shed in time to give the next customer a perm.

"Cassidy—" Sara Kramer got out of her car. "Your yard is looking quite festive."

"The snowman is new," Cassidy said.

"I don't remember seeing the igloo last year."

Igloo? "What igloo?"

Sara motioned behind her. "The igloo on the other side of the trailer."

Cassidy hadn't bothered flipping the blinds this morning before she'd opened her hair salon for business. "Hmm…Make yourself comfortable." She strolled around to the front of the trailer, then stopped and stared. "Wow." A huge blow-up igloo sat in the yard, an extension cord leading to Betty and Alice's trailer.

"Isn't it cute," Betty said from her porch.

Cassidy liked the little penguins guarding the entrance. "Where did you and Alice buy this?"

"We didn't."

Logan again?

"Woke up around midnight and heard someone making a racket outside," Betty said.

Cassidy hadn't heard a thing.

"We gave Logan permission to plug the cord into our trailer." Alice joined the group.

Tears stung Cassidy's eyes, but she braved a smile. *Ah, Logan. What are you trying to tell me?*

"You shouldn't keep the igloo plugged in all day. I hate to see your electric bill increase," Cassidy said. Before her neighbors asked too many questions…"Gotta run."

"Will you be at the Sanders' hoedown tonight?" Sara asked when Cassidy entered the shed.

Good Lord, how had she forgotten Junket's annual Christmas barn dance? "No, I plan to stay home and relax." Last year's party had been a disaster because Bethany had died the afternoon of the dance.

Two hours flew by and Cassidy finished Sara's perm, then sent her on her way. Left alone with her thoughts she worried how Logan intended to pass the anniversary of his wife's death. An image of him sitting alone at home or in a bar popped into her mind. She hurried inside and phoned his ranch. The answering machine clicked on.

"Logan. It's me, Cassidy." Pause. "I saw the igloo." Pause. "It's really big." She chuckled. "The inflatable penguins are cute."

Then she sucked in a steadying breath. "Why don't you come over tonight? We'll watch a movie or play cards." Fearing she'd bungled the invitation, she said goodbye and hung up.

The last client of the day left at five. Cassidy cleaned the shed, locked the doors, then plugged in the Christmas lights and waited for the phone to ring.

Logan's not going to call.

With a heavy heart she made supper, threw a load of clothes in the washing machine and watched TV. At eight Cassidy settled her mother in bed for the night with a stack of magazines and her favorite hand cream, then stepped outside and stared at the igloo.

What are you doing, Logan? Where are you?

"Cassidy. Is everything all right?" Alice's voice drifted through the dark.

"I was thinking of Logan. Today's the one-year anniversary of his wife's death."

"Oh, my. That's right." Alice placed her palm against her heart. "Why don't you go check on him, dear? He shouldn't be alone tonight."

"Mom's already in bed."

"Betty and I will be right over."

Grateful for the chance to see Logan, Cassidy changed into a turquoise sweat suit, brushed her teeth, dabbed on a touch of makeup and pulled her hair into a ponytail before driving off.

Fifteen minutes later her heart sank as she parked next to Logan's truck in front of the dark ranch house. A growl greeted her ears when she climbed the porch steps. Twister lay near the swing.

"Quiet." She stamped her foot as she'd seen Logan do and the snarling stopped. Cassidy knocked twice.

Waited. Knocked again. She turned the knob and the door swung open.

"Logan?" She paused in the entryway while her eyes adjusted to the darkness. "Logan, are you home?"

The sound of a bottle being opened drifted down the hallway. *Please don't let him be drinking.*

She crept down the hall, then felt along the kitchen wall for the light.

"Go away, Cassidy."

Her fingers flipped the switch.

Logan sat at the kitchen table hunched over a bottle of…*root beer*.

He looked so lost sitting alone at the table.

"I don't want company," he mumbled. "Especially yours."

She felt his pain down to her soul and wanted to help—but how? She sniffed.

His head jerked around. "Don't."

She marched across the room to the refrigerator.

"What are you doing?"

"Making sure you eat."

"I'm not hungry."

"I don't care." He would not bully her into leaving. She removed a package of lunch meat, stale sandwich rolls, sliced cheese and ranch dressing.

"Cassidy, I'm not in a good mood." His words wobbled with emotion.

"I knew that before I drove over." She buttered the bread, then placed the slices into the toaster oven at the end of the counter. The timer dinged a minute later. She set the sandwich on the table, then pulled out a chair and sat.

He stared at the food. "I almost forgot about Bethany's

accident today." His quiet admission exploded through the room.

"It's okay, Logan." She squeezed his fingers.

As if her touch scorched his skin he hissed and yanked his hand free. "A husband doesn't almost forget the day his wife and unborn child died." The words were punctuated with an icy glare. After a tense stare-down he broke eye contact and muttered a four-letter word.

Her presence agitated Logan more than helped, but she couldn't bring herself to leave him in this condition. She jumped up from her seat, grabbed the rag in the sink and scrubbed at an imaginary stain on the counter.

"You know what?" he said.

Bracing herself, she faced him. "What?"

"This is your fault."

Her fault?

He pointed his finger at her. "You're the reason I'm in such a funk."

Before she realized his intent, Logan left the table and clamped his hand around her arm. He tilted her chin until their mouths almost touched.

"I forgot why today was so important because you're stuck in my head. Since the minute I got out of bed this morning all I've thought about was kissing you. Dancing with you. Holding you." His lips brushed against hers. "I can't get you out of my head." Then his mouth crushed hers, his tongue demanding entrance. Forget sweet and romantic. The kiss was desperate and punishing.

Then the kiss turned apologetic—his lips softened, cajoled, and his tongue toyed with hers, teasing. Cassidy lost herself in Logan's embrace, desperately trying to ignore the voice in her head reminding her that his attraction to her was tangled in a strong desire to keep her and the baby safe. As long as she understood the fire she ignited in him had nothing to do with tender feelings for her, she could protect herself from heartbreak.

Oh, Logan. She sighed, unable to stop her fingers from sifting through his hair. One strong hand caressed the nape of her neck while the other slid over her hip to cup her bottom, pressing her gently against his arousal. He massaged her sensitive breast, thumbing the nipple until it ached. His hand left her fanny and slipped beneath the hem of her jacket, brushing her slightly rounded tummy.

His body turned to stone. Not even a breath escaped his mouth. The warmth in his brown eyes cooled. He released her and retreated across the room. "I can't do this." His chest heaved when he sucked in a gulp of air. "Leave, Cassidy." It wasn't a request but an order.

Lord, how she wished she was enough to ease his pain, but no matter what she said or did, nothing would bring his wife and child back to life. "You shouldn't be alone tonight."

"Leave. Please."

Cassidy hesitated. What if Logan lost himself too deeply in grief that he'd never found his way to being a father?

"If you don't leave, I will," he threatened.

His solemn ultimatum propelled her from the room, down the hall and out the front door.

TWO HOURS AFTER Cassidy left the house, Logan lay in bed, staring at the water stain on the ceiling. The numbers on the nightstand clock flipped to 11:00. A cool breeze fluttered the bedroom curtains.

Cassidy. Cassidy. Cassidy.

Why had he sent her away? When he'd held her and kissed her he'd felt forgiven. Exonerated. The past forgotten. The future nowhere in sight. But the future stared him in the eye and he needed to focus on the important stuff—keeping Cassidy and the baby safe.

Night after night since Cassidy had informed him about the baby he'd woken from sleep drenched in sweat, gasping for breath—Bethany's car crash vivid in his mind. Each nightmare was the same—he'd run to the mangled vehicle only to discover *Cassidy's* bloody body crumpled in the front seat. There would be no sleep tonight until he apologized for his Neanderthal behavior and made sure she was okay.

Twenty minutes later Logan pulled into the Shady Acres park and eased the truck over the first speed bump. He slowed to a stop in front of Cassidy's trailer and stared in shock at the chaos unfolding before him.

Cassidy's mother wandered around the yard in her pajamas pulling the Christmas lights down and trampling the decorations. The igloo lay on its side, two penguins deflated. The candy canes had been scattered across the lawn and Rudolph was missing his blinking red nose.

Logan hopped out of the truck and scanned the side yard—no sign of Cassidy, but at least her mother hadn't wrecked that part of the yard. Either the older woman was sleepwalking or had left the house without Cassidy knowing. He stopped at the edge of the walkway and listened to her ramble.

"Who did this?" She tugged on the lights Logan had wrapped around the porch rails. Losing interest in the now sagging strands, she focused on the potted poinsettia at the bottom of the porch steps. "I don't like flowers." She kicked over the pot, spilling dirt on the sidewalk.

"Hey, Sonja. What are you doing?" Logan asked quietly, hoping not to startle her.

She jumped, then scowled. "Who are you?"

"Logan Taylor. Cassidy's friend."

"Did you put this junk in my yard?"

"No, ma'am. Cassidy did. She likes to decorate for Christmas."

Sonja frowned. "I need to put these away."

Good God, how did Cassidy deal with a situation like this? He glanced at the trailer but the windows remained dark. "Why don't I help? You sit and rest." He led her to the porch steps. Her skin felt cold to the touch, so he removed his jacket and put it around her shoulders. Once he was certain she'd remain seated, he went to work repairing the damage while keeping a conversation going in hopes that Sonja would forget about the decorations.

"Did you like your job at the fertilizer factory, Sonja?" He didn't know anything personal about the woman other than where she'd worked most of her life and that she'd never married Cassidy's father.

"I hated the smell." She pointed to the igloo. "Did you put that thing in my yard?"

"Yep."

"It's ugly."

If he didn't change Sonja's mind about the decorations she might come out tomorrow night and do more damage. *She's got Alzheimer's, idiot. She won't remember any of this.*

"Hey, Sonja. I like those candy canes you bought at

the store the other day." He held his breath hoping her mind would play along.

"What candy canes?" She searched the yard, her gaze passing over the broken canes.

"Right here." He bent down and examined the two halves of one cane. Restringing the lights tighter might hold the pieces together.

"I bought those?" Sonja asked.

"You said Cassidy would like them." He felt foolish for lying and for treating the older woman like a child. He couldn't imagine having to speak to his mother this way.

"Cassidy likes those?"

"She sure does."

"Then why did you break them?"

He swallowed a groan. "I, uh, tripped."

"You better fix them or Cassidy's going to cry." Sonja's voice wobbled and she wrung her hands.

Great. Now he'd upset the poor woman. Right then the trailer door opened. "Mom? Are you—" a gasp echoed through the night air as Cassidy surveyed the wreckage.

"I'll fix it all, Cassidy. You don't have to worry about—"

"Logan?" Cassidy noticed him for the first time. "What are you doing here?"

"I came to apologize for—" he glanced at her mother. "And to make sure you were okay." He sucked in a deep breath. "You were pretty upset when you left my place."

Ignoring her mother's "I don't know how this happened," Cassidy descended the porch steps.

In a trance she wandered around the yard. She picked up Rudolph's nose and her shoulders slumped. At the sight of her dejected silhouette the immensity of Cassidy's situation sunk into Logan.

He pulled her close, tucking her head beneath his chin. "It's going to be all right, honey."

Her cold lips brushed his neck.

"It's chilly and your mom's been out here for a while. Why don't you help her to bed. Tomorrow morning the yard will be good as new. I promise."

"Thank you." Feet dragging in the grass as if each step took effort she approached her mother, then held out her hand. "Let's go back to bed, Mom."

"I'm tired, Cassidy."

"Me, too, Mom."

The door closed and Logan swallowed the knot in his throat. Caring for her mother was taking a toll on Cassidy. He was embarrassed and ashamed that earlier tonight he'd added to her burdens. Standing in the middle of Santa's playland, Logan came to the realization that he could no longer remain uninvolved in Cassidy's life. Whether he liked it or not, whether she wanted it or not, he intended to carry some of the burden before Cassidy wore herself out.

"THAT SHOULD DO IT." Logan shoved the screw driver into his tool belt.

He'd dropped by Cassidy's to install bells on both the front and back doors. He'd suggested the measure so that if her mother woke in the middle of the night and tried to leave the trailer the bell would ring and wake Cassidy.

"Thanks. This was a good idea." She hated admitting she needed help. She'd been positive she could handle her mother, cut hair and raise a child. Last night her mother had proved her wrong. She glanced at the clock. Almost suppertime. "Are you hungry?"

"I'm good. Why don't you take a quick nap while I fix the faucet." He nodded to the water dripping from the spigot in the kitchen sink.

Maybe dinner could wait a half hour. "If you're sure…" She glanced at the doorway leading to the family room.

"Don't worry. Your mom will be fine with me."

"Wake me if she becomes difficult." Cassidy drifted to sleep as soon as her head hit the pillow. The tantalizing smell of garlic and warm bread dough woke her at seven-thirty. *Seven-thirty!* She rolled off the bed, used the bathroom and hurried into the kitchen.

There sat her mother and Logan eating pizza. His eyes softened when they landed on her and she self-consciously smoothed a hand over her messy hair.

"Just in time." Logan rose from his seat, pulled out a chair for Cassidy, then went to the cupboard and removed a glass. "Water or milk?"

"Water, please." She yawned. "Hi, Mom."

"Cassidy, this nice young man cooked dinner."

Maybe she was still groggy. Maybe she hadn't gotten over the shock of her mother's antics last night. Or maybe her hormones were out of whack. Whatever the cause, Cassidy's eyes watered and darned if she could stop the tears.

Logan set the water glass in front of her, then crouched at her side and brushed a strand of hair from her eyes. "What's wrong?"

"Nothing." She flashed a weak smile and Logan returned to his seat. "How's the pizza, Mom?"

"Fine." She pointed across the table. "Your friend made us supper."

When Cassidy noticed Logan had cut her mother's pizza into small pieces the tears came harder.

"Sonja? How would you like to eat supper and watch one of your shows?" Logan asked.

"Oh, that would be nice." Sonja left the table, her napkin falling to the floor.

"Hang on," Logan said. He carried her mother's plate and drink into the other room and switched on the TV for her.

"Sorry if I overstepped my bounds," he said, joining Cassidy at the table. "You were conked out when I checked on you and—"

"I needed help." The words almost choked her. She wanted his love, too, not just his help.

They ate in silence. Logan finished first, pushing his plate aside. "I have something to say, but I don't think you're going to like it."

If his serious tone was any indication she *knew* she wouldn't. "I'm listening."

"Until last night when I saw your mother destroying the Christmas decorations I hadn't realized how difficult your situation was. I think—"

"You think I should put my mother in a home?"

"That's not what I was going to suggest." He strummed his fingers on the table. "I want you to stop cutting hair."

"What?" Was he crazy? She needed the income to make ends meet.

"I can help with expenses and—"

"No, Logan. I won't take your money."

"Think of it as a child support payment."

"There is no child…yet."

"You can't keep going like this, Cassidy. It's not good for you or the baby."

She admitted she was burning the candle at both ends but she hated being backed into a corner. Was this how Logan felt when she'd told him about the baby?

He carried his dishes to the sink, rinsed them and then put them in the dishwasher. "Will you at least consider decreasing your work hours cutting hair?"

"This is my busiest time of year. The tips pay for Christmas presents." And her after-Christmas shopping spree.

His mouth drew into a thin line and his shoulders stiffened. "If you won't accept my money, then I'll have to help you out other ways."

Other ways? She was afraid to ask what he meant.

Supper finished, Cassidy rose from the table only to be instructed to relax in the living room with her mother. Logan cleaned up the kitchen, went outside and turned on the Christmas lights, then he insisted Cassidy soak in the tub.

"Mom needs her—"

"I'll keep your mother company." He turned to Sonja. "How about a game of cards?"

"Oh, I love card games."

Her mother couldn't remember how to play any card games, but instead of sticking around and warning Logan, Cassidy retreated to the bathroom and did as Logan suggested—soaked in a bubble bath. An hour later Cassidy put her mother to bed.

She expected Logan to take off but he elected to stay.

They watched the late-night news together and he gave her a foot rub.

Cassidy closed her eyes and sighed in contentment. She could get used to Logan's pampering—if only it came from the heart and not from a feeling of obligation.

Chapter Six

The Junket holiday parade took place each year the Saturday before Christmas. Logan hadn't planned on attending but when Cassidy mentioned taking her mother he decided he'd better tag along in case Cassidy needed help.

He and Cassidy stood on the curb outside the barber shop and Sonja sat in one of the two lawn chairs Logan had stowed in the truck. The day had dawned bright and clear but the midmorning temperature hovered near fifty and folks lining both sides of the street wore jackets and gloves. The parade was only two city blocks long but lasted almost an hour due to the floats rolling by at three miles per hour. Baker's Drugstore offered free coffee and hot chocolate for the event and Helga served it up from a beverage cart in front of the store.

Logan had hoped to run into Fletcher and his son, but his friend was nowhere in sight. Maybe he and online Daisy were off sight-seeing. As soon as the 4-H Fair kid passed by with his winning ewe, Logan jogged across the street to the drugstore.

"Hello, Logan," Helga said.

He nodded. "Two hot chocolates, please."

"Are you enjoying the parade?"

"Yep." In truth, he'd rather be watching a movie in Cassidy's trailer. He didn't mind crowds, but since Bethany's death most people steered clear of him—not that he blamed them. Logan hadn't been in the mood for shooting the bull with anybody. Now that he'd shown his face in public again he surmised people were keeping their distance because they'd heard Cassidy was carrying his baby.

"How are things between you and Cassidy?" Helga handed him one hot chocolate.

"Fine." Logan wished the woman would hurry up. He didn't want to appear rude, but he had no intention of discussing his love life.

Helga's gray eyebrows arched. "Are you and Cassidy planning to marry?"

Marry? "I don't—"

"Who is that cowboy across the street cozying up to Cassidy?"

What cowboy? Logan spotted a ranch hand from Fletcher's spread chatting with Cassidy. The guy said something and Cassidy laughed, then playfully punched the man in the arm.

How come she never laughed like that around him?

Because you never joke with her. Right then the high school marching band playing "Jingle Bell Rock" entered the parade procession. Logan shouted his "thank you" to Helga, then turned to cross the street but discovered the band blocked his way.

Jealousy gnawed his gut as he watched the ranch hand flirt with Cassidy. Whatever they were discussing sure tickled her funny bone. He hadn't seen her smile this much since…since never.

As soon as the band passed by, Logan shuffled to the other side of the street. He handed Cassidy and Sonja the hot chocolates.

"Logan, have you met Dale Richards? He works out at the Rocking J," Cassidy said.

"Not officially." Logan shook hands with the man, then wrapped an arm around Cassidy's shoulders. "Cold?" he asked her, then leveled a she-isn't-available glare at the cowhand.

Dale frowned. "Are you two a couple?"

"We're friends," Cassidy said a little too quickly.

"In that case—" Dale grinned "—how would you like to drive to Midland for lunch and a movie tomorrow?"

"She can't." Logan tightened his hold around Cassidy.

Her eyes widened. "I can't?"

"No, remember." *Play along with me, Cassidy.*

She refused. "Remember what?"

His brain scrambled for a reason she couldn't go out with Dale. "The picnic."

"What picnic?" Darned if a smile didn't flirt with the corner of her mouth. *She's toying with you.*

"The picnic at my ranch."

"Oh, that picnic." Cassidy apologized. "I'm sorry, Dale. Maybe another time."

Another time? Not if Logan had anything to say about it.

"Enjoy the parade." Dale moseyed along and struck up a conversation with another cowboy.

"Care to explain the Neanderthal routine?" Cassidy asked.

"No." As a matter of fact Logan wasn't sure what had gotten into him. He'd thought he wasn't ready for a romantic relationship but the idea of Cassidy falling in love with another man felt wrong. But anything more than friendship with her meant risking his heart and taking responsibility for another human—two humans. Three including Sonja.

If he didn't ask Cassidy to marry him, then the only thing he knew for certain was that one day some other guy eventually would. Could he live with that? He was damned if he did and damned if he didn't.

Cassidy tugged his sleeve. "So what time's the picnic?" she asked, calling his bluff.

"Noon." That gave him just over twenty-four hours to figure out the future—his and Cassidy's.

PLUMES OF DUST ROSE in the air as the red compact drew closer. A sense of déjà vu swept through Logan. Had it only been eleven days since Cassidy had shared the news with him that she was pregnant? In such a short time she'd worked her way beneath his skin.

Don't you mean months?

Cassidy had passed in and out of Logan's thoughts since the September night she'd rescued his drunken carcass from the honky-tonk. For months he'd convinced himself that their romp between the sheets meant nothing, but in truth—she'd gotten to him.

Granted his feelings for her were a jumbled mess. He liked her. Desired her—that was for sure. But love her? No matter how tempting, he didn't dare.

After parking the car next to the barn, she flashed a smile at him and his libido shot off the charts. She hadn't said a word and already his body hummed like a fine-tuned motor. No woman had ever had that effect on him before.

Twister barked. Logan stamped his boot against the ground and the dog slunk into the shadows.

Logan approached the car and rescued the lunch basket from Cassidy's hand. Today she wore jeans and a fluffy pink sweater. She looked soft and huggable. "We're picnicking in the hayloft."

"I've never been invited up into a hayloft by a handsome cowboy." She batted her eyelashes.

The little flirt. "Then it's time you were." He grasped her hand and led her inside the barn, then hesitated at the bottom of the ladder. "Maybe you shouldn't climb up there in your condition."

"I'm not an invalid. I'm pregnant."

As if he needed a reminder. He steadied the ladder and she ascended the first few rungs, then he followed, thoroughly enjoying the view in front of him.

"Oh, this is nice." Cassidy surveyed the hay bales he'd pushed together and spread a quilt over. An oil lantern cast a cozy glow about the dimly lit area.

She opened the basket, then handed him a fried chicken leg before claiming a spot on the blanket. "Guess what I learned this morning?"

"What's that?" He contributed two water bottles from the cooler he'd stashed in the loft.

"Thanks to you I won the Shady Acres Christmas decorating award." She pulled a blue ribbon from her pocket. "See."

"I bet you win the award every year."

Her cheeks turned pink. "Usually the Millers and I

switch off winning, but this year the inflated igloo clinched the deal for me."

"Glad I helped." He dug into the chicken. Cassidy handed him a napkin. After wiping his mouth he took the plunge. "Cassidy, I'm worried how you're going to cope with a newborn, your mother and keeping up with your hair-styling business."

"I'll manage."

Her answer disappointed him. He'd believed his showing up at Cassidy's trailer the past few nights had proved she couldn't manage on her own and needed his help. Confused, he attacked another chicken leg.

"I saw Fletcher with a woman earlier today." She brushed the pad of her thumb against the corner of his mouth and Logan felt a zap shoot through his body. "Crumb," she said. "The woman looked familiar but I don't recall having seen her around town before."

"If it's who I think it is, then she's not from Junket." Obviously Fletcher had been ignoring Logan's calls because he was busy pursuing his new love interest.

"Who is she?" Cassidy asked.

"Fletcher met the woman through his MySpace page."

"I've considered setting up a MySpace page." She opened a container of pasta salad and passed Logan a fork. "But I don't have the time to fool around with that stuff."

Thank God. At least he didn't have to worry about Cassidy hooking up with some online stalker or weirdo. "We need to discuss the future." This morning in the shower he'd convinced himself that he should marry Cassidy to protect the baby from being labeled a bastard. The possibility that one day Cassidy might get a better offer from another man had nothing to do with his decision. Or so he'd told himself.

"What about the future?"

No sense pretending he was a great orator. "I've changed my mind about the baby." He waited for a smile. Maybe a squeal. Even a hug. Anything that suggested Cassidy was happy about his announcement.

"Changed your mind how?" The guarded tone in her voice was no less than he deserved.

"I want the baby to have my last name."

"Fine. I'll make sure Taylor is on the birth certificate."

She wasn't making this easy. "That's not what I meant." He sucked in a deep breath and took the plunge. "I think we should get married."

Silence—the loud, heavy kind that weighed down a man's conscience filled the confines of the loft. "I think we should—"

"Heard you the first time." And it wasn't what Cassidy had hoped to hear. She offered him a second chance to get this right. "Why do you think we should get married?"

"You're going to need help, Cassidy. Help with the baby. Your mother."

Pain gripped her heart in a bear hug. Logan had proposed not because he loved her, but because he was apprehensive about her and the baby's well-being.

"It's the perfect solution," he said.

"Solution?" The word leaked from her mouth in broken syllables.

"Marriage has its privileges." He tugged a strand of her hair and winked.

Sex. Guilt-free sex. She supposed a man who'd been

married as long as Logan had wouldn't feel comfortable in a long-term relationship without a commitment. But marriage in exchange for bedroom privileges and help around the trailer didn't interest Cassidy.

What about love? She was twenty-eight years old and had never been in love before. She didn't need Logan to give their baby his name. She didn't need Logan to protect her from the gossipmongers. She didn't need Logan to help her make ends meet or watch over her mother.

She needed him to love her.

Cassidy shook her head. "I won't marry you."

"But—"

"I won't marry you, Logan, because you don't love me." No sense admitting she'd already fallen in love with him. She had her pride.

"Why do we have to complicate things with love—" He pulled her to her feet and hauled her against him "—when we have this between us?" He kissed her, his tongue sweeping her mouth, begging her to participate. She didn't have the strength to resist him. He palmed her breast, drawing a moan from her. No denying it…Logan set her on fire.

The kiss gentled, ending with small nibbles on her lower lip. "I've never felt this strong of an attraction to any woman, Cassidy. Why can't we be together without emotions getting in the way?"

"Because I need more than great sex, Logan. I need love."

"You're asking for the impossible from me." His voice shook.

She stroked his cheek. "It's okay, Logan. No one

would ever blame you for not wanting to take a chance on love again." Cassidy had hoped…prayed she was the woman to coax this man to risk his heart again, but it wasn't meant to be. "I'd better go."

His arms tightened around her for a fraction of a second before he released her. In silence she packed the picnic basket and he helped her down the ladder. Neither spoke as he walked her to the car.

She drove away, watching Logan's solitary figure in the rearview mirror. He looked so alone. So lost. All the love he needed in the world waited for him in her arms…if only he'd give her and their baby a chance to heal his wounded heart.

LOGAN PULLED UP to Cassidy's trailer at two in the morning and stared at the deflated igloo, which lay on the grass in a puddle of plastic.

He hadn't meant to hurt her.

When she'd left his ranch earlier in the afternoon, he'd tackled every chore that had been on his to-do list for the past six months, counting on physical exertion to ease the pain of Cassidy's rejection.

Hours later Logan had entered the empty house and had been hit with the realization that he was really, truly alone. Exactly what he'd wanted…needed after Bethany's death—isolation and emptiness. Each day had been a big, black void and that's how he'd managed to survive.

Until Cassidy happened along and ruined it all.

She'd made him admit that he didn't want to be alone anymore.

After a shower Logan had gone to bed, expecting to

pass out. Sleep eluded him. He'd lain wide awake, alternately cursing and praising Cassidy. Why wouldn't she give him—them—a chance? Why did she need him to be something he couldn't? To offer something he didn't have to give?

If he knew what was good for him, he'd stop obsessing and move on. *To what? More of the same depressing loneliness?* He wanted one more chance to explain. *Two in the morning isn't the best time to plead your case.*

He considered leaving but a light switched on inside Cassidy's trailer. A moment later, she stepped out the door wearing a bathrobe and big fuzzy slippers. His throat tightened. He wanted to wake up to Cassidy every morning and see her this way.

She descended the porch steps and approached the truck. He leaned across the seat and opened the passenger door. She hopped in. He didn't utter a word, even though hundreds clamored inside his head. Then she whispered, "Trouble sleeping?"

"Yeah. You?"

She nodded.

He yearned to hold her. Kiss her. "Cassidy. I feel things for you that I shouldn't." She remained silent and he was grateful that she allowed him to bungle his way through without interrupting.

"I care about you. I like you. You made me smile when I thought I had nothing left to smile about." He grabbed her hand and squeezed tight. "But you scare me."

"You're afraid of me?"

"I'm afraid of falling in love with you." Every time he was with Cassidy, he felt like he was fighting to keep his head above water. "I loved Bethany and our baby and they died."

"You're hurting, but—"

"You have no idea how…" He released her hand and leaned against his door. "The pain…the guilt… it's beyond anything you've ever dealt with in your life."

"Love and pain go hand-in-hand, Logan. When you love someone, there's always the potential for hurt."

"If I allow myself to love you and the baby and then…" He was unable finish the morbid thought.

"Logan." She scooted closer and clasped his face between her hands. "Don't you see? It's too late. You already care."

"I never said I didn't care. Why else do you think I went to the doctor's appointment with you? I had to know that you'd get there safely. That the same thing wouldn't happen to you that had happened to Bethany on that road." She shifted to her side of the front seat. The two feet separating them might as well have been the entire state of Texas.

"Let me be with you in my own way," he pleaded.

"I can't."

"Why?" he rasped.

"Because I love you. And I won't settle for anything less than a fairy-tale ending." She pressed a kiss to his cheek, got out of the truck and went inside the trailer.

Cassidy loved him—just not enough to accept him the way he was.

DRIZZLE GREETED CASSIDY Monday morning. The weather matched her mood. Christmas Eve was three days away and she'd never been more depressed by the thought of spending the holiday without Logan. How two people cared for one another yet were unable to find a way to be together was beyond her.

She stared out the dining room window and tears burned her eyes. The igloo rested in a crumpled heap on the ground. She loved Christmas decorations. Now they'd always be a sad reminder of what could never be with Logan. Next year she'd be darned if she'd string up a single strand of lights.

With a sigh she turned away from the window and tackled morning chores while her mother slept. As she tidied the hall bathroom, sadness shifted to anger. How had Logan believed for one minute that she'd accept a marriage proposal that excluded a love-until-death-do-they-part clause?

Granted most people didn't understand the responsibilities of caring for a loved one with Alzheimer's, but Logan hadn't even considered how a change in their relationship would affect her mother. Had he assumed Cassidy would pack her things, move to the ranch with him and leave her mother behind in the trailer?

Did he have any idea how attached her mother had become to certain things, like her recliner? How Cassidy didn't dare buy a new TV because a new TV came with a new remote and her mother would have fits figuring out how to operate the device. Her mother knew what cupboard the drinking glasses were in. That the grape juice bottle was stowed on the second shelf in the refrigerator. And the silverware drawer was to the right of the sink.

If Cassidy changed her mother's surroundings all

hell would break loose. To put herself and her mother through that much stress for an I-care-about-you marriage proposal wasn't fair. What if six months later Logan decided he was tired of her mother's shenanigans? Or that the baby took all Cassidy's time and energy, leaving little left over for him? Would he just quit their marriage?

Without honest, true love they'd never survive the ups and downs of married life, raising a family and coping with her mother's illness. Her love for Logan wasn't enough to justify putting herself, their baby and her mother through heck and back.

She paced in front of the refrigerator, then paused to study the ultrasound picture of the baby—their son. *I wish we were enough to convince your father to risk loving again.* But no one could fix Logan save himself.

After a quick breakfast of jelly toast and orange juice, Cassidy headed outside to open the shed for business. No matter that the bottom had dropped out of her world, she'd paint on a happy face for her clients and pretend life was grand.

Mrs. Wilson pulled into the driveway around nine. Cassidy didn't remember seeing the woman's name on the schedule. "Hi, Mabel. Do you have an appointment today?"

"No, no." Mabel stared.

"What's wrong?" Cassidy asked.

"Are the rumors true?"

Good grief. Back to that again? "Yes, I'm carrying Logan's baby."

"Not that rumor. Is it true you turned down Logan's marriage proposal and broke that cowboy's heart?"

Cassidy gasped.

"You didn't!" Mabel paced the confines of the shed. "Maybe it's not too late to fix things."

Fix things? "Who told you Logan proposed?"

"Francine called this morning and said her nephew, Scott, who's home from college for Christmas break, worked the night shift at the Quick Stop. Logan gassed up at three in the morning, then went inside to buy a coffee. Scott mentioned that Logan looked like he needed a stronger drink than coffee and that's when Logan confessed he'd had his marriage proposal flung back in his face."

Flung! "There was no *flinging* involved when I declined Logan's proposal."

"He's the father of your baby."

Tears burned Cassidy's eyes. "It's complicated."

"Come here." Mabel sat on the loveseat.

Cassidy gave in to the need to share her grief. If her mother was of sound mind she'd have cried a river on her shoulder already. "I love him. I swear I do."

"Then why won't you marry him?"

"He doesn't love me."

Mabel's eyes widened. "He said so?"

Cassidy nodded. "He's afraid he'd never survive if he loved me and our child and then we suffered the same fate as Bethany."

"That man needs a good kick in the pants."

"I agree." Cassidy wiped her runny nose on her sleeve.

"Logan must care about you if he proposed."

"He cares, but I want more. I want love."

"You know what I think?" Mabel said.

"What?"

"He won't be able to stop himself from falling in love with you after you're married."

"He's pretty determined." Logan owned the patent on stubborn.

"How can he not fall in love with you when he's with you every day and you and he make love every night?"

Cassidy blushed at the frank talk.

"I'm old, Cassidy, but I'm not dead. Although Buford drives me insane half the time, he and I have a very good relationship in the bedroom. Women can deny it all they want but sex keeps a marriage together." Mabel offered a gentle smile. "Love makes it magic."

"But what if after all that he still doesn't love me?"

"Have faith, young lady. One day Logan will wake up and realize he can't live much less take his next breath without you."

Cassidy really wanted to believe that. She'd never know if she and Logan were meant for a happy-ever-after if she didn't at least try. Could she do any less for their child? "Thanks, Mabel. I'll think about what you said."

"Good." The older woman stood. "I expect a wedding invitation to arrive in the mail well before that baby of yours is due." Mabel got into her car and drove off.

If there was one thing Cassidy knew for certain, it was that marriage or no marriage, she'd always love Logan.

LOGAN HEARD the phone ringing inside the house as he climbed the porch steps Tuesday afternoon. He wasn't in any rush to answer—mostly because he didn't care who it was or what they wanted. As a matter of fact, Logan hadn't given a crap about anything since Cassidy had declined his marriage proposal.

The answering machine clicked on when he entered the kitchen.

"Logan, it's Mabel Wilson. What on earth is the matter with you?"

Huh?

"How can you expect a woman to accept your marriage proposal when you don't tell her you love her?"

Ah, jeez. The college kid at the Quick Stop must have run off at the mouth.

Logan pulled a chair out from the kitchen table and sat. He had a feeling the retired schoolteacher was about to unload on him.

"Cassidy loves you, Logan. You'd be a fool to walk away from her and the baby because you're a scaredy cat."

Scaredy cat? She had no cause to speak to him like a third grader.

"Everyone knows how devastated you were when Bethany and the baby died."

No, they don't.

"But life goes on. You can sit on the sidelines and wallow in self-pity or you can get off that stubborn arse of yours and live again."

The answering machine shut off. Five seconds later the phone rang. Logan let the machine pick up.

"Good grief, can't a woman finish reprimanding a man before she's hung up on?"

How much more did the old bat have to say?

"Don't be afraid, Logan. You and Cassidy are perfect for each other."

The dial tone buzzed, then the machine clicked off.

Logan was tempted to consider Mrs. Wilson's advice but his brain ached from all the pondering he'd done the past twenty-four hours. He got up from the table and fixed himself a glass of water. The phone rang again.

"Logan, this is Mrs. Hildebrand."

Mrs. Hildebrand? Why the heck was the mayor's wife calling?

"I'm at Cassidy's—"

Logan lunged for the phone. "Hey, Mrs. Hildebrand."

"Oh, good, you're home, Logan. Is Cassidy with you?"

"She's not here."

"I arrived for my hair appointment but the shed is locked and her car is gone."

Logan glanced at the calendar and his heart stopped beating. A red circle was drawn around Tuesday December 22. "Cassidy has a doctor's appointment today." Damn, he'd forgotten.

"Do you know when she's supposed to return?"

He'd written 10:00 a.m. on the date. He glanced at his watch. It was three now. Where was she? Panic churned in his gut. "Mrs. Hildebrand, I'll see if I can track her down."

"Tell Cassidy to call me when she has a minute and I'll reschedule my appointment."

"Sure thing." Logan hung up, grabbed his wallet off the counter and tore out of the house.

Dear God, please let Cassidy be okay.

Chapter Seven

"Why are we sitting here?" Cassidy's mother asked for the tenth time in as many minutes.

"Because the car broke down," Cassidy answered yet again.

Lord help her. She needed to figure a way out of this jam. They'd only been stuck on the shoulder of the road a short while, but already her patience with her mother was wearing thin.

Since Betty and Alice had left for Galveston on Sunday, Cassidy had brought her mother along to the doctor's appointment today. After receiving a clean bill of health from Dr. Gilda, Cassidy had treated her mother to lunch at a restaurant, before heading back to Junket for Cassidy's three o' clock hair appointment.

Twenty miles outside of town the car's motor had suddenly quit. Steering had become impossible and Cassidy had barely managed to guide the hatchback onto the shoulder of the road. "Stay in the car, Mom." Cassidy checked for traffic—not one vehicle had passed since they'd become stranded—then got out of the car.

She raised the hood and poked around the engine. No

burning-oil or leaking-fuel smells. Then she noticed the broken belt. *Shoot.* They definitely needed a tow.

"Stay put, Mom," she said when she opened the driver's side door. "I'm walking up the road a ways to see if I can get cell phone coverage." She reached over the front seat and grabbed one of the magazines she kept in the car. "Read this."

"Oh, thank you, honey."

Cassidy walked half the length of a football field, then flipped open the phone. *Drat.* She recalled the popular cell phone company ads on TV and decided she and her mother were stuck in one of those dead-zone scenarios. She stared at miles of flat, dry land. *Damn, where was the network when you needed it?*

As soon as she returned to the car her mother asked, "Are we leaving?"

"No, Mom."

"I have to use the bathroom."

Great. Cassidy had suggested visiting the ladies' room before they'd left the restaurant in Midland, but her mother had refused. She rummaged through the glove compartment and removed a sanitary hand wipe. "You'll have to squat in the gully."

"Cassidy! Someone might see."

If they were lucky. "Then you'll have to..." She squinted at the speck of color growing in the distance. "Help has arrived." She stood in front of the raised hood and waved her arms. The vehicle was a green cargo van. "Hey!" She jumped up and down. "Stop!" The van whizzed past. The driver hadn't even tapped the brake lights. *Jerk.*

Okay, new game plan. She'd driven past a bar a half

Marin Thomas   103

mile back. She and her mother would have to hike there and use the phone to call for a tow.

"Grab your purse, Mom. We're going for a walk."

"I don't want to walk. I want to go to the bathroom."

"That's where we're going—to the bathroom."

"Okay."

Breathing a sigh of relief that her mother decided to cooperate, Cassidy helped her out of the car and guided her along the shoulder of the road.

You wouldn't be in this predicament if you'd called Logan last night and reminded him of the doctor's appointment.

True. But Logan would have insisted on driving her into Midland and she hadn't wanted to speak to him until she'd made up her mind whether or not she'd accept his marriage proposal. "Guess what?" she said. "Logan asked me to marry him."

"That's nice, dear. Who's Logan?"

"You know Logan. He comes over every night and helps around the trailer. Watches TV with you." *Remember.*

"Oh, that Logan."

How many Logans did her mother think there were?

"I'm in love with him, Mom."

"That's nice, dear."

"But he can't let go of Bethany and I don't know if I want to take a chance on a man who *might* one day learn to love me."

When her mother didn't respond, Cassidy asked, "Did my father love you?"

"Juan was a sweet boy."

"Where did you meet Juan?" Cassidy asked.

"The corner market. He ran with a wild bunch and

my parents warned me away from him. He was a handsome man."

Her mother rarely had trouble remembering events that happened years ago, but ask her yesterday's weather and she'd draw a blank.

"I stayed out all night with him and the next morning my suitcase sat on our front porch and the door was locked."

"Your parents kicked you out?" Cassidy couldn't imagine doing that to her child.

"I was a bad girl, Cassidy."

Her mother had never mentioned this incident. "Where did you go?"

"Juan's mother took me in. I lived with her until I graduated from high school and had the baby."

The baby being Cassidy. "Why didn't you marry Juan?"

"He liked another girl better."

Her father was a schmuck. Most days Cassidy was glad she'd never met her father. She had nothing good to say to him, especially after witnessing her mother struggle to raise a child without the help of a husband or family.

Logan isn't anything like your father. Logan wanted to accept responsibility for their child—and her. But Cassidy didn't want to be his responsibility. She wanted to be the love of his life.

He cares for you.

Of course he did. Otherwise he wouldn't have helped her with her mother or bought her the yard decorations. Or asked her to marry him.

"Where are we going?" her mother asked.

"There's a bar around the bend in the road." Cassidy pointed up the highway.

"Why are we going to a bar?"

"So you can use the bathroom."

"I don't have to go to the bathroom."

Cassidy bit down on her tongue to keep from groaning aloud. "We're almost there." Another five minutes of walking and Larry's Lounge came into view. The place was a dive.

The bar, which had existed since Cassidy had been a little girl appeared to be pieced together with mismatched sheets of rusted aluminum siding. License plates from all over the U.S. decorated the front door along with a lopsided Christmas wreath. Music drifted from the open windows. Three trucks and two motorcycles sat in the lot.

Holding tight to her mother's hand they entered the joint.

Cassidy was pleasantly surprised by the clean interior. The open windows allowed fresh air to circulate, which made the cigarette smoke almost tolerable. The cement floor was sticky but there were no puddles of beer or bodily fluids.

Catcalls rang out when the patrons noticed the newcomers. Ignoring them, Cassidy headed for the bartender, a short balding man. "Hello. I'm Cassidy and this is my mother Sonja."

"Name's Joey."

"Where's Larry?" Cassidy asked.

"Larry's dead. Didn't see much use in changin' the name of the place. What can I do for you, ladies?"

"My car's stranded up the road and I need to call for a tow."

Her mother tugged Cassidy's sleeve. "I have to use the bathroom."

"Phone's by the restrooms." Joey pointed across the room.

"Thanks." Cassidy led her mother to the pink door painted with a silhouette of a large-breasted woman. They both took care of business in record time, then Cassidy sat her mother at the bar and ordered her a glass of red wine.

"One of them—" Joey set the wine in front of Sonja, then motioned to a group of men playing cards in the corner "—might be able to give you a lift to town."

No, thanks. "That's all right. The tow-truck driver will take us to Junket."

"Sheriff Sanders stops in after his shift around six."

Six o'clock was two hours away. She glanced at the half-emptied wine glass. Her mother would be drunk by then.

Cassidy dug out her wallet and set a ten-dollar bill on the bar. "Refill her glass." She slipped away and inserted three quarters into the pay phone. Dialed information and added another dollar's worth of quarters for the operator to connect Cassidy to a towing service. The tow company took her credit card number over the phone and promised to have someone be at the bar within an hour.

"What's the hangdog face for?" Joey asked when Cassidy slid onto a stool.

"It's been a long day." She was in no mood for a five-cent therapy session with a honky-tonk bartender.

"Git old like me and you'll be wishin' for long days."

Oh, what the heck. "Car troubles are the least of my worries. The father of my baby proposed, but he doesn't love me."

Joey frowned. "Well, that's a damn sight better than the father of your baby runnin' off with another woman."

"I love him." Cassidy sighed. "But he's afraid to love me."

The bartender set a glass of water in front of Cassidy. "On the house."

"Thanks."

"Love's a fickle thing," Joey said.

"Any advice on how to help him overcome his fears?"

"Yeah, but it ain't fittin' for your mama's ears."

"Care to dance, ma'am?" An older man wearing leather biker chaps, black combat boots, a tie-dyed T-shirt and a bandana secured around his forehead stood behind Sonja's stool.

Cassidy opened her mouth to decline the invitation, but her mother spoke first. "I'd love to dance."

Biker man helped her mother from the stool and led her to the jukebox where they looked over the songs.

"Clarence is harmless," Joey said. Then he asked, "Was the baby a surprise?"

"Yes." Her cheeks warmed.

"One-night stand?"

Startled, she asked, "How'd you know?"

"Happens to the best of us." Joey dug out his wallet and removed a photograph.

"She's adorable." The little blond girl wore a tiara and a pink ballet suit.

"Jenny was six in that picture. She's fifteen now. Her and her mama live in Georgia."

"Did you marry Jenny's mother?"

"Nope."

"But…"

"I should have." He shrugged. "Cheryl wanted us to try and be a family, but I figured somethin' better was waitin' for me 'round the corner."

"And was it?"

"Still waitin'." Joey slipped the picture into his wallet.

There was no telling what the future would bring for Cassidy and their child. Bethany's death had taught everyone that life was short and sometimes bad things happened to good people. If Cassidy didn't take a chance on marrying Logan would she end up like Joey—still waitin' with only regrets to keep her company?

LOGAN PICKED UP SPEED as he passed the city-limit sign for Junket. He prayed Cassidy had decided to spend the day in Midland shopping and that's why she'd missed Mrs. Hildebrand's hair appointment. His conscience refused to consider any other reason.

His stomach twisted with guilt. He'd been too caught up in his own emotional crisis that he'd forgotten Cassidy's doctor visit this morning.

She could have reminded you.

No. If there was one thing he'd learned about Cassidy in the short time they'd been together it was that she possessed a boat full of pride. Shame rose like bile in Logan's throat. He'd trampled Cassidy's pride with his halfhearted marriage proposal.

Mrs. Wilson's call replayed in his mind. He had clung to the past, afraid to let go of Bethany and the baby. Because if he did, he'd have to forgive himself for not driving his wife to the doctor's appointment the day she'd been killed in a head-on collision.

A moment later he spotted a car on the side of the

road—Cassidy's red hatchback. She wasn't sitting in the front seat or standing next to the vehicle. A cold chill washed through his body

This can't be happening again.

He checked the rearview mirror, slowed the truck and swung across the oncoming lane, then parked on the shoulder in front of the hatchback.

The raised hood obviously meant engine trouble. He walked around the car, searching for damage that would indicate the vehicle had been involved in an accident. The absence of dings and dents failed to reassure him.

How long had Cassidy been stranded? Where was she now? Had someone stopped to help her? He shielded his eyes against the sun's glare and scanned the area. "Cassidy!" he shouted. The wind hurled her name back in his face.

She either caught a lift from a passerby or walked somewhere for help. Sweat popped out across his forehead when he thought of the risks involved with both scenarios.

Where would she find help? He stared down the road, then remembered the bar around the bend. He got in his truck and sped down the highway. Less than a minute later he parked in front of Larry's Lounge. Years ago he and Fletcher had stopped for a beer at Larry's. The place hadn't changed much since then—it was still a dive.

Logan entered the bar and immediately his ears winced at the ZZ Top song blasting from the jukebox. He scanned the clientele, his heart clenching when he spotted Cassidy—no worse for wear—chatting with the bartender. Relief swept Logan like a twister through the plains, scattering his emotions to smithereens.

What a fool he'd been to believe he could marry Cassidy and not fall in love with her. No matter how often he told himself that what he felt for her was not love…Right here. Right now. His heart said otherwise. Logan was in love with Cassidy Ortiz. She was his future. His destiny. His road to forgiveness.

The song ended. Heads turned in Logan's direction. Eyes watched. Ears listened. Then Cassidy swiveled on the bar stool and their gazes connected. Damned if his feet wouldn't budge. He opened his arms. *Give me another chance, Cassidy.*

She zigzagged between tables and chairs, then launched herself at him. Once he wrapped her tight in his embrace, Logan decided then and there to stop fighting his love for this woman.

"I'm sorry, Cassidy." He nuzzled her hair. "Sorry for not remembering the doctor's appointment today."

"I should have called to remind you."

He had so much more to say, but fear blocked the words from leaving his mouth.

"I called a tow," she said. "The guy should be here in a few minutes. But it's nice of you to try to rescue me." She flashed a saucy smile.

Cassidy had it all wrong. She had rescued him. "We need to talk."

"I know. Let me get Mom."

"Your mother's here?" He scanned the room and spotted Sonja drinking with an older man at a table in the corner.

"She's having the time of her life." Grasping his hand, Cassidy led Logan outside, away from prying eyes. "I want you to know that I understand—"

He pressed a finger against her lips. "I've been afraid to love you, Cassidy. Afraid something bad would happen to you like it did to Bethany and the baby. I've cared for you. Been attracted to you since this past September. But not until I saw your car stranded on the side of the road a few minutes ago with you nowhere in sight did I finally admit to myself that I've fallen in love with you."

"Oh, Logan."

"When I spotted the hatchback, I wasn't thinking about the baby. Only you. It's too late for me to save Bethany or the baby—"

"I don't need to be saved, Logan."

The muscle along his jaw pulsed, but he didn't break eye contact. "You're right. You don't need saving. If there was ever a woman more capable of taking care of herself, her mother and a child that woman would be you."

After sucking a deep breath he continued. "You might not need me, but I need you, Cassidy. I want to be your forever man. And I want us to raise our baby together and be a family." He kissed her tenderly.

"I fell in love with you the night you strung Christmas lights on my trailer and bought that goofy inflatable snowman." She put his hand on her stomach. "Your *son* and I can't replace Bethany and the child you conceived together, but I promise we'll love you just as much and we'll be the family you always dreamed of having."

"My son?"

She smiled. "We're having a boy."

Logan hugged her and their Christmas baby close. What he'd believed had been the worst mistake of his life—sleeping with Cassidy that fateful September night they'd met at Billie's Roadhouse—had turned out to be his own personal Christmas miracle.

Maybe there really was a Santa Claus after all.

* * * * *

MARRY ME, COWBOY

Chapter One

"How come you never said anything about this date with MySpace Daisy when I helped you pull the bull out of the mud bog?" Logan Taylor's voice echoed in Fletcher McFadden's Bluetooth headset late Friday morning.

"Figured I'd end up canceling on her," Fletcher said. In truth he was nervous as all get out. Online Daisy seemed like a nice woman, but what if she turned out to be a troll? "Dress slacks or jeans?" Fletcher studied the rows of shirts, jackets and pants hanging in his closet.

"Your divorce hasn't been final a year," Logan said. "Are you ready to date again?"

"We both know my marriage was doomed from the beginning, but I was…never mind." A one-night stand had resulted in a pregnancy and Fletcher had taken responsibility for his actions by tying the knot with Sandi. Although they weren't in love with each other he'd been determined to make the marriage work and he hated that he'd failed.

"Everyone's entitled to a mistake." There was an odd catch in his friend's voice before he cleared his throat.

Oh, hell. What would Logan know about screwing

up? The guy had married his high school sweetheart and they'd been happy until her death. At least his buddy had experienced true love. Fletcher had a rotten track record in that department.

Logan had been the first person Fletcher had confided in when he'd arrived home early from a business trip and had walked in on Sandi and her lover in the bedroom. What he hadn't confessed to Logan was that his wife had been sleeping with the guy off and on during their entire seven-year marriage. Fletcher figured it was payback for having cheated on his teenage sweetheart.

He and Darla Baker had dated all through high school and the pressures of their senior year—deciding what college to go to, applying for scholarships and financial aid had stressed their relationship. They'd agreed to take a breather from each other until after final exams. He'd screwed up and had gotten caught—by Darla's best friend Sissy—making out at the drive-in movie theater with another girl. That ended his relationship with Darla for good.

In hindsight he'd been a moron in his marriage also—the clues had been right in front of his nose. Sandi's frequent overnight shopping excursions with so-called out-of-town friends. The time he'd discovered she'd continued taking her birth control pills after they'd agreed to have another baby. If there had been one thing in his miserable marriage to be grateful for it was that Sandi hadn't contested the divorce. She'd agreed to a handsome settlement and Fletcher received sole custody of their son.

"This woman know you're stinking rich?" Logan interrupted Fletcher's stroll down memory lane.

"She thinks I'm a used-car salesman."

"You're kidding."

"Nope." Fletcher grinned at the mirror hanging on the closet door. "Pretty clever, eh?" He figured if Daisy discovered he and his father owned a successful bull-breeding business, she'd be all over the McFadden fortune and not Fletcher's sweet ol' self.

"Where are you and this Daisy hooking up?" Logan asked.

"Why all the questions? I called for wardrobe help."

"I ought to charge you for my help. First, the bull and now I'm picking out your clothes."

"We're meeting at the drugstore in less than an hour."

"Is Daisy from around here?"

"She lives in Midland." Fletcher hoped he and Daisy would hit it off. He was in the market for a good-time-no-strings-attached affair. After screwing up with Darla, then marrying Sandi for all the wrong reasons, Fletcher was done with serious relationships. And he had Danny to consider. His son was having a hard time adjusting to Sandi's absence and the last thing Fletcher wanted to do was cause him more trauma by bringing another woman into their lives. "Back to my outfit."

"Jeans and a white dress shirt. No tie. Sunday boots."

"Thanks, hoss."

"What's Daisy look like?"

"Blonde. Big hair. Lots of makeup."

"Texas Mary Kay gal, huh?"

"I guess."

"What if she didn't post her real picture online?"

"If she's as pretty as the back end of a mule, I'll cut the date short." The past four months he'd corresponded with three women. If Daisy didn't work out, he'd arrange a date with the next one on his list.

"Did you post a picture of your ugly mug on your page?"

"Of course."

"Good luck, buddy."

"Hey, Logan. What do you say we get together Christmas Day?" Logan's father had died six years ago and his mother lived in Florida with Logan's aunt. Fletcher hated the idea of his friend sitting home alone the first Christmas without his wife.

"I'll think about it. Later, Romeo."

The dial tone buzzed, then Fletcher's earpiece went silent.

"Dad! Where are you?"

"In here."

His seven-year-old-son dashed into the room and launched himself onto the bed. Danny looked nothing like Fletcher. There was little of the McFadden Irish in the kid. He had his mother's blond hair, slight build and brown eyes. Fletcher didn't care. Despite the fact that his son had been conceived during a momentary loss of sanity on Fletcher's part he'd loved the boy the moment he'd been born.

"Whatcha doin'?"

"Getting ready for a—" He didn't want Danny worrying about his father dating, so he lied. "Trip into town."

Danny jumped on the mattress, raising his arms above his head to touch the ceiling fan. "Can I come?"

"Nope." His son had woken with a bellyache this morning—a medical condition that had become all too frequent since the divorce and Sandi's absence. "If you're too sick to go to school, you're too sick to leave the house."

"I'm feelin' better now."

Yeah, I bet you are. "Maybe next time."

"I'm bored," Danny whined.

"Quit jumping." He reinforced the command with a glare. "Practice your spelling words with Grandpa." After the divorce Fletcher had sold the house he and Sandi had built in a subdivision on the outskirts of Midland and moved back to his father's ranch. Danny appreciated the extra attention and in truth Fletcher needed his father's help in dealing with his son's unruly behavior.

"Can I go fishing with Grandpa if I get all my words right?"

"Yeah." Probably the wrong answer but Fletcher felt bad that his numerous attempts to convince Sandi to pay more attention to their child had failed.

"Thanks, Dad!" Danny raced from the room.

Fletcher tucked in his white dress shirt, aligned his belt buckle with his jean zipper, shoved his feet into high-polished black Laredo boots, donned his Stetson, then squirted on cologne. He studied his image in the mirror. His looks weren't special—not like his buddy, Logan, whose movie-star face stopped women in the street. At six three, Fletcher had height on his side and a strong physique from a life of ranch work, but his auburn hair and ruddy face were nothing to brag about. *Hope you like what you see, Ms. Daisy.*

The ride into Junket took fifteen minutes. He stopped at the only intersection in town and had trouble peeling his foot off the brake. *Chicken.* Hell, yes he was scared.

He hadn't had a date—a real date—in seven years. What did women expect from men these days? Dinner and movie before…sex? Speaking of sex…it had been so long since he'd done the hanky panky he wasn't sure he remembered how to seduce a woman.

A horn honked and he checked the rearview mirror. Old man Carson sat behind the wheel of his 1978 Ford truck. His hunting dog Beau occupied the passenger seat. Carson didn't go anywhere without Beau. Maybe Fletcher should get a dog instead of a woman. Dogs might smell bad but they were loyal critters. He lifted his foot off the brake and continued down Main Street.

Paying no attention to the town's new Christmas decorations, his eyes scanned the vehicles parked outside the local businesses. Daisy said she drove a black Volkswagen Beetle. No Beetle in sight so he parked in front of Baker's Drugstore and shut off the engine.

He considered hiding in his truck until he spotted a big-haired blonde, but decided the polite thing to do was to wait for Daisy inside the store. Mrs. Polanski was towel drying glasses behind the soda fountain when he walked through the door. He slid onto a stool and greeted the gray-haired woman. "Afternoon, Mrs. P."

When Mrs. P. and her husband moved to the area and purchased the drugstore from Darla's parents, the older woman had learned the name of every child in Junket and knew which parents in the community struggled to put food on the table. Whenever those children dropped by the drugstore Mrs. P. handed out free hot dogs and glasses of milk.

"How's Danny, Fletcher?"

"Woke up with another stomachache this morning."

"He misses his mother."

Fletcher agreed, although he didn't understand how a child missed a mother who'd hardly paid attention to him since his birth. He suspected Danny worried his father might desert him, too. Every day Fletcher expressed his love to his son, but the words failed to reassure the boy.

"Did you drop by to eat or chat?" A blue-veined hand wiped the counter with a damp rag.

"I'm meeting a friend." Then he added, "You haven't seen a strange woman wandering around here, have you?"

Mrs. P. nodded toward the front of the store. "She doesn't look familiar."

He swiveled on his stool and his eyes collided with… "Darla?"

"Hello, Leonard. How's the used-car business?"

No. No way.

Had she played him for a fool and strung him along all these months? "Daisy?"

The corner of her mouth tilted. Damn if she wasn't struggling not to laugh. "Sorry, I'm not your Daisy."

He frowned. "Then how did you know—"

"A coworker has a MySpace page and found a used-car salesman named Leonard from Junket, Texas. She wondered if I knew you."

Well, damn. This was embarrassing. "What brings you back to town after all these years?" Wow, she looked great. Better than she had in high school.

"Sissy's new baby, Emma, is being baptized on Sunday and I'm her godmother."

Sissy Keller—the name made Fletcher shudder. The woman had blistered his ears when she'd caught him cheating on Darla at the drive-in.

Before the next question left his mouth, the drugstore door opened and in walked a Texas Mary Kay disaster. Fletcher swallowed hard as he took in the woman. With her big-boned body and wide hips, his blind date could wrestle a swamp gator and come out on top.

Daisy towered over Darla's five-seven height. The woman's blond hair stood a half foot taller than in her MySpace photo. And he sure hadn't remembered that big mole on her chin. Daisy smiled and Fletcher cringed at the ruby-red lipstick smudges on her teeth.

"You wouldn't happen to know a Leonard Reynolds, would you?" Daisy asked Darla.

He moved out of the shadows. "That would be me."

Daisy turned at the sound of his voice and her mouth sagged open. "But…but…"

But what? He moved forward and held out his hand. "I'm Leonard." No sense telling her his real name when he intended to cut the date short.

She stared at their entwined hands. "I thought you were…"

"Were what?" Jeez, the woman had trouble getting her words out.

"I thought you'd be…smaller."

Was that disappointment he heard in Daisy's voice?

Smiling, Darla disappeared around an end cap. "What do you mean, smaller?" he asked.

Daisy waved her hand, drawing his attention to the costume jewelry adorning her fingers—fake emeralds and rubies. "I don't care for men who are bigger than me."

A snicker came from the next aisle over. Instead of being embarrassed that Darla was eavesdropping, Fletcher was relieved he hadn't impressed Daisy.

"I guess you want to cancel our date," he said.

"Ah…" Daisy sighed. "I'm sorry, Leonard."

"Sure. Okay." He shrugged.

Daisy paused with her hand on the door. "You're not upset, are you?"

"No, why?"

"I don't want you to stalk me on MySpace or say bad things about me on the Internet because I hurt your feelings."

"I'm not that kind of guy."

"Well, it was nice meeting you, Leonard. Sorry things didn't work out."

"Likewise," he said, relief surging through him. Now that Daisy was out of the way he could concentrate on Darla.

AS SOON AS FLETCHER'S MySpace Daisy left the drugstore, Darla emerged from her hiding place in the next aisle.

"Whew. Close call," he said.

Twelve years and a failed marriage had aged Fletcher—lines fanned from the corners of his green eyes and threads of silver mixed with the auburn hair at his temples. Older…but still handsome. Cowboy handsome. Rugged, masculine.

For a moment she lost herself in his gaze and the years melted away. Her mind retreated to the days they'd sat at this very soda fountain and planned their future. The sound of a throat clearing chased away the memories, leaving Darla shaken.

"You two ordering anything to eat?" the older woman behind the counter asked.

"Sorry." Fletcher grasped Darla's hand. "Mrs. P., this is Darla Baker."

"Herb and Mary's daughter?"

"Yes, ma'am. Darla, this is Helga Polanski."

Darla tugged her tingling fingers free. "Nice to meet you."

"Likewise, dear. Your parents sure gave us a good deal on the store. We'll always be grateful for their kindheartedness." She lifted a pot from the warmer. "Coffee's on me." After filling two cups, she said, "I'll be in the stockroom if you change your mind about lunch."

"Thank you." Darla slid onto a stool. Fletcher's scent, a familiar cologne, competed with the aroma of strong java. She sipped the hot brew, counting on the caffeine to settle her nerves. She'd hoped to avoid running into Fletcher this weekend and now here she sat drinking coffee with the man.

"You're staring." She wasn't a woman prone to perspiring but Fletcher's gaze burned into her skin.

"You've changed," he said.

The appreciative sweep of his eyes over her figure caused her heart to hiccup. After her last relationship had ended, she'd finally shed the extra fifteen pounds she'd gained during college and had carried around since. She'd hoped a new Darla would attract a different kind of man—one she could see herself marrying and spending the rest of her life with.

"Seriously, Darla. You look great."

His compliment soothed the old wound Fletcher had inflicted on her eons ago. A small part of her—the young girl who'd believed the sun rose and set on

Fletcher's broad shoulders was pleased he'd approve of her new image.

He tapped her bare ring finger. "This surprises me."

Darla's boyfriend had caught her off-guard this past spring and proposed. Blake was a nice man, but in many ways boring. He'd asked her to wear his ring for a month and then give him an answer. She'd agreed. Thirty days later she'd said *no*. One failed relationship wouldn't have been a big deal, but Blake's proposal had been the third Darla had declined since graduating from law school.

"I came close—" She wiggled her fingers. And in case he believed she'd pined for him all these years, she added "—a few times."

Darla had been surprised when her coworker showed her Fletcher's MySpace page. His photo had unlocked all the feelings for the man—both good and bad—that resided in her heart all these years. The shock of that discovery led her to believe that her commitment issues with other men were tied to her unresolved feelings for her first love.

She'd thought she'd gotten over Fletcher's betrayal. After high school graduation she'd left for college in Austin and he'd gone to school in Lubbock. Many times through the years she'd thought about him. Wondered where he was and who he was with. She'd discovered that old feelings die hard and she'd believed it best to spend as little time as possible in Junket to avoid running into Fletcher. She'd been relieved when her parents had sold the drugstore and moved to Nevada and she no longer had a reason to return to town. Then Sissy had called with the news she was pregnant with her first child and wanted Darla to be the godmother. After all these years Darla finally came home.

"I like your hair." Fletcher possessed that country charm missing in metropolitan men. When they'd dated, the bull breeder's son had found something nice to say about her every time they were together.

"Thanks." The short bob was a drastic change from the waist-length hair she'd worn in high school and college. But her hairstyle wasn't the only thing that changed. She wasn't the same small-town girl who'd grown up in Junket. Attending college, then living and working in Dallas had curbed her Pollyanna views.

His twinkling eyes sobered. "So what do you do for a living?"

"I'm a lawyer."

"You went to law school?"

The awe in his voice claimed her achievements impressed him. "I'm a lawyer for the Environmental Protection Agency in Texas."

"That's great."

"I heard you're divorced." Sissy had sent Darla a copy of the *Junket Journal*'s front-page story on the divorce. Darla had felt genuinely sorry for Fletcher at having his and Sandi's dirty laundry aired in such a public way. The newspaper had been another reminder of her love-hate relationship with small-town life.

"Been almost a year since Sandi and I split," he said.

"You two have a son."

"Danny. He's seven."

Darla had been in her first year of law school when her mother had phoned with the news that Fletcher and Sandi had had a little boy. The first twenty-four hours Darla had been numb. The second devastated. The third miffed. The fourth indifferent. On the fifth day the cycle repeated itself.

For years she'd held on to hope that one day she and Fletcher would end up together—Danny's birth had ended that fantasy. Three failed engagements later, Darla began to suspect she'd only been fooling herself into believing she was over her first love.

"Does your son live with you?" she asked.

"Danny and I moved back in with my dad. It's worked out well since Mom passed away and—"

"I was sorry to hear about your mother." Darla had thought the world of Marilyn McFadden. She had sent a sympathy card and flowers, but hadn't returned to Junket for the funeral.

"Dad likes having us around and I'm grateful for his help with Danny." Fletcher shrugged. "The boy's a handful."

Jealousy reared its ugly head. She'd expected to be a mother by now. As a matter of fact she and Fletcher had agreed on three children when they'd mapped out their lives in high school. Her gaze clashed with his in the mirror behind the fountain and the sadness dulling his green eyes snatched her breath. Did Fletcher harbor a few regrets of his own? Before she had a chance to ask, the drugstore door opened.

Like a strong gust of wind a child blew inside, knocking over a holiday candy display. The cacophony echoed through the store and Darla pressed a hand to her lips to keep from laughing as the blond-haired boy stared slack-jawed at the scattered tins rolling in every direction.

Mrs. Polanski appeared, hands pressed to her cheeks as she surveyed the mess.

"I'm real sorry, Mrs. P." The boy dropped to his

knees and began collecting tins. "I didn't mean to bust your shelf."

"Not to worry, Danny. We'll get things cleaned up in no time."

Danny? Darla glanced at Fletcher who groaned and rubbed his brow.

"Hey, Dad." The boy waved his arm wildly.

"Did I mention my son is a distant relative of the Tasmanian devil?" Fletcher said.

Stomach twisting into a painful knot, Darla braved a smile. Danny McFadden looked nothing like his father and everything like his mother, Sandi Rutledge.

"What are you doing here?" Fletcher met his son in the middle of the aisle.

Danny ignored the question and peeked around his father. "Who's that?" The scowl on the child's face took Darla by surprise. Joining the males she held out her hand. "I'm Ms. Baker. Pleasure to meet you, Danny."

The boy reluctantly offered his hand, then yanked it away as soon as Darla clasped his fingers.

"Where's Grandpa?" Fletcher asked.

"At the bank. He said I could come in here and get some gum."

"Finish helping Mrs. Polanski clean up this mess." Fletcher turned away and was unaware of the dark glare Danny sent Darla.

She wanted to reassure the child she had no intention of intruding into his life or laying claim to his father. Instead, she said, "I have to get going." She'd stopped by the drugstore to buy a gift for little Emma's baptism, but running into Fletcher and his son had shaken her and she needed fresh air.

"Stay for lunch," Fletcher said.

She forced herself to make eye contact. "Sissy's expecting me. I have to go."

"How long are you in town for?"

"Until Monday."

"I want to see you this weekend."

"I…" She clenched her hand into a fist.

"For old time's sake?"

Although she'd never admit as much—Fletcher interested her more now than he ever had. Green eyes simmering with heat, he inched closer, forcing her to tilt her head to maintain eye contact. *Oh, my.* Was he…

"Are you gonna kiss that lady, Dad?"

Fletcher's head jerked and his cheeks reddened.

Thank goodness Danny had interrupted them or she would have made a huge mistake and kissed Fletcher back.

"Have dinner with me," he whispered.

No denying the chemistry between them was still there. Dare she spend more time with Fletcher?

Dinner might lead to a kiss, which might lead to…

Or dinner might lead to finally being able to put Fletcher behind her once and for all.

"Yes, I'll have dinner with you."

Chapter Two

"Who's this strange woman Danny says you were talking to in the drugstore earlier today?" Fletcher's father came out of the house and stopped next to the built-in grill on the patio where Fletcher cooked fajita meat.

Right then Fletcher's phone vibrated. He checked the number—Logan. No doubt his buddy was curious about the meeting with Daisy. Wait until Logan found out Fletcher had run into Darla at the drugstore. He let the call go to voicemail.

"It's a long story, Dad."

His father helped himself to a beer from the mini-fridge built into the outdoor kitchen. "I'm listening."

Refusing to go into the MySpace details, Fletcher cut to the chase. "Darla Baker's back in town for the baptism of Sissy Keller's new baby on Sunday."

"Darla was at the drugstore?"

His high school girlfriend was a sore subject between father and son. Daniel McFadden had loved Darla like a daughter and had been disappointed when the young couple went their separate ways following high school.

"What's she been up to all these years?" his father asked.

"She's an EPA lawyer for the state of Texas and lives in Dallas."

"I'll be darned."

Darla's law degree had taken Fletcher by surprise. She'd brought up the subject of becoming a lawyer when they'd dated but he hadn't believed she'd been serious. If things had worked out between them would she have gone on to law school and put marrying him on hold after graduating from college?

"Single, divorced or married?"

He should have known his father wouldn't be satisfied until he'd heard Darla's life story. "She was engaged—" he left out *a few times* "—but things didn't work out." He wondered why. He'd have thought a hot shot corporate CEO or doctor would have snatched Darla up long before now.

Maybe she's not over you.

Yeah, right.

The Darla that had walked into the drugstore didn't have to settle for a man like him—a country boy who was boring in the handsome department. With her looks and career she could snag any guy she wanted. He and his father's wealth attracted a fair share of interest from the opposite sex, but Darla didn't need his money. The Lexus he'd watched her drive away from the drugstore in had proven that.

Anxiety twisted Fletcher's gut. It had taken a long time to put Darla behind him. Now she was back, stirring up old memories and feelings. He never expected to have an opportunity to seek her forgiveness for what he did in high school and he didn't want her to head back to Dallas before he told her how sorry he was.

Forgiveness? Go ahead and tell yourself that's the reason you want to spend time with her while she's in town. Face it, you think she's hot.

There wasn't much left of the small-town girl—that was visible anyway. She'd shed the girl-next-door look. And Fletcher was intrigued with the new grown-up Darla—sophisticated, sexy and confident.

"What does she look like now?" His father's question grabbed Fletcher's attention.

Sexy. "She wears her hair short." And her blue eyes reminded him of a cloudless sky.

"You attracted to her?"

"That's a little personal, Dad." His ex-wife couldn't hold a candle to Darla's stylish hair, trim figure and sophisticated clothes.

"I'd say it was damned important if you intend to get back together."

"You're jumping the gun." Fletcher didn't know where this thing with Darla would lead. Shoot. She had a life and a career in Dallas. His father was too old to handle the bull business by himself so Fletcher was stuck in Junket. Besides, Danny was his first priority and the last thing his son needed was his father bringing another woman into the family who might end up leaving them.

"I'd like to visit with her. Find out how her parents are doing."

"She's coming over for supper tonight." He glanced at his watch. "Should be here in a half hour."

"Why didn't you say as much?" His dad tossed the

empty beer bottle in the recycle bin. "I'll make your mother's famous cold bean salad." The back door slammed in his wake.

After Fletcher's mother died Daniel McFadden had refused to hire a cook or maid. His father hadn't wanted a strange woman taking over what Marilyn McFadden had once called her domain. Good thing Fletcher knew how to grill meat. Most nights he threw a piece of beef on the cooker while his father microwaved a vegetable. Tonight he'd planned on serving fajitas with Mexican rice. *And cold bean salad.*

Danny joined him outside. "Grandpa says I can't go to soccer practice 'cause we're having company for supper."

"You can't go to soccer practice because you stayed home sick from school today." His son played on an intramural co-ed soccer team. After today's practice the team would take a recess until after the Christmas break. Danny wasn't all that great at the sport, but Fletcher had encouraged him to join the team, hoping that for a few days a week the practices and games would take his young mind off his parents' divorce.

"I want you to be on your best behavior tonight with Ms. Baker," Fletcher warned.

Danny climbed onto a stool at the bar and twirled. "Is she the lady I saw at the drugstore?"

"Yep. We're old friends." In truth, Fletcher didn't know what he and Darla were anymore. Old friends? Old lovers? Old enemies?

"I don't like her. She looks mean."

Mean? "Ms. Baker's a nice lady."

"You're grumpy. Did Grandpa yell at you?"

Deep breath. Exhale slowly. Danny's headstrong

attitude put Fletcher's patience to the test on a daily basis and he found deep breathing worked best to release tension. "Go ask Grandpa if you can help with the bean salad."

"He told me to help you."

"Then—" Fletcher caught himself before the words *stop bugging me* escaped his mouth. He wished he knew how to handle Danny better. The school counselor had recommended a therapist after Sandi split. For three months Fletcher had driven Danny into Midland for therapy. Fletcher had participated in a few of the sessions, but in the end there had been little progress in Danny's disposition. He hoped with time and love, his son would settle down. "I could use a clean plate to put the meat on."

"Okay." Danny hopped off the stool and dashed into the house. Fletcher worried he'd made a mistake in inviting Darla out to the ranch for dinner. He should have suggested a restaurant, but he knew his father would enjoy seeing her.

"I let myself in. Hope you don't mind." Darla's voice reached his ears and he spun.

The sight of her brought a smile to his lips and chased away his doubts. He set the tongs aside and turned down the flame. "Did you bring dessert?" He motioned to the shopping bag in her hand.

She held out the bag and he peeked inside.

German chocolate cake. Darla hadn't forgotten his father's favorite dessert. That had to mean she still…what? Cared? "You look nice." She smelled nice, too. The sultry scent she wore was a far cry from the cheap dime-store stuff he'd given her for Valentine's Day one year.

"I didn't pack any jeans for the trip." She rubbed a hand against the black dress pants that hugged her curves.

He pictured Darla in tight jeans and his mouth watered.

"Hey, Dad." The back door banged against the house for the third time. "Here's the…" His voice trailed off when he spotted Darla.

"Hello, Danny. It's nice to see you again." Darla held out her hand and Danny gave her the plate.

"I'll take that." Fletcher set the plate by the grill, then passed off the shopping bag to his son. "Give this to Grandpa and tell him that Ms. Baker's here."

Solemn-faced, Danny did as he was told, smacking the bag against the edge of the doorway when he went inside the house—probably on purpose.

"What can I get you to drink?" Fletcher motioned for Darla to sit at the bar.

"Wine, if you have it."

"Sure do." He poured her a glass of red and helped himself to a beer. "How's life in Dallas?"

"Great." Her smile didn't give a clue how great. "I own a condo downtown and I love standing on the balcony at night and seeing the skyline illuminated by the city lights."

"Sounds like you prefer a faster pace of life?" Fletcher had traveled with his father on numerous bull buying trips around the country but they'd mostly visited ranches and bypassed metropolitan areas.

"I didn't like the city at first," she confessed. "But the hustle and bustle grows on you. There's plenty to do in your free time."

"Are you insinuating that Junket is boring?" He grinned.

"It is what it is, Fletch."

He liked that she used his nickname—made him feel as if a few intimacies remained between them. "You've got to miss something about your hometown."

Her gaze slid across his face and settled on the grill behind him. She shrugged. "Now that Mom and Dad are living in Nevada there isn't much here for me anymore."

Her words sliced through Fletcher. "I should have guessed you'd study environmental law," he said. In high school, Darla had been the president of the science club. "Remember the bungled experiment that—"

"That fire—" she pointed a finger at him "—was Lonny's fault, not mine. He tipped over the Bunsen burner." They chuckled at the memory.

"Darla Baker," Daniel McFadden's voice boomed through the screen door seconds before he stepped outside.

Grateful for the interruption, Darla slipped off the stool and hugged the older man. She hadn't wanted to discuss her career or her last-minute decision to enter law school after learning Fletcher had married Sandi.

"You're all grown up, young lady."

Darla's smile faded. "I'm so sorry about Marilyn."

"You would have been proud of her. She fought the cancer right to the end." Daniel blinked away the sheen in his eyes. "Marilyn loved yellow roses. We put your bouquet on her grave after the funeral."

Darla should have done more than send a card and flowers. She should have returned for the funeral. But at the time she hadn't the strength to face Fletcher, Sandi and their two-year-old child.

"Bean salad ready, Dad?" Fletcher asked, ending talk of his deceased mother.

"Table's set." Daniel motioned for Darla to follow him inside and Fletcher trailed with the fajita meat. Nothing had changed since she'd last visited the McFadden home. The same blue-and-white checked valance hung across the kitchen window…the cow cookie jar on the counter…the antique crock filled with dusty cooking utensils.

The kitchen table had been set for four—the familiar blue stoneware bringing back memories of all the meals she'd shared with the McFadden family. She'd spent as much time in this house as she had at her parents' home. "What can I do to help?"

"Suppose you can fill the water glasses," Daniel said. "Danny boy drinks milk."

Fletcher set the meat platter on the table. "Excuse me, while I track down Danny boy."

Daniel chuckled. "That rascal sure is a handful."

"He seems like a nice boy." The compliment was difficult to offer and that bothered Darla, but the boy reminded her of another broken dream of hers—having children with Fletcher.

"Danny's an active kid, but since the divorce he's been a troublemaker."

"Divorce is tough on kids," she said, treading on unfamiliar ground.

"My grandson might behave better if his mother paid more attention to him." Daniel was a man who didn't mince words. "She gave up full custody of Danny and didn't bat an eye. Hardly ever sees the boy. Never calls."

Guilt flooded Darla that she'd harbored even the tiniest bit of jealousy toward Danny. The poor kid had been all but abandoned by his mother. Darla appreciated the not-so-subtle reminder that Danny was an innocent victim and had nothing to do with how things had worked out between her and Fletcher.

Unsure what to say, she mumbled, "I guess some women aren't cut out to be mothers." Any further discussion of Sandi's failure at motherhood was nixed when Fletcher escorted Danny into the kitchen with a hand on the back of the boy's neck.

"What happened?" Daniel pulled out a chair and sat at the table. Everyone followed suit.

"It was an accident, Grandpa." Danny's gaze bounced between his father and grandfather.

"He broke the ceiling fan in my bedroom," Fletcher said.

"Your dad's told you a million times not to jump on the bed and grab at those blades." Daniel passed a plate of warmed tortillas to his grandson.

"My hand got caught." The boy's face reddened with embarrassment.

Sympathy for Danny caught Darla unprepared and she blurted, "I cracked my mother's antique flower vase." All three males stared at her in surprise. "I played ball in the house with our dog. Bandit knocked over my mother's favorite flower vase and it broke."

"Did you get in trouble?" Danny asked.

"Yep. I said I tripped over Bandit and bumped into the table. When my mother vacuumed the rug she found Bandit's ball beneath the couch and knew I'd been playing catch with the dog."

"Did you get punished?"

"Yep. But not because I broke the vase. Because I lied about how I broke it."

"The truth is always best," Fletcher said.

Danny stared at Darla and the gleam in his eye told her he was up to no good. He reached for his milk and at the last second Darla's hand shot out just as Danny tried to tip over the glass. She smiled. "Oops."

The boy's mouth dropped open, then he snapped it shut and scowled.

"I've been meaning to ask how the bull business is going, Daniel," Darla said.

The tension at the table eased. Daniel McFadden loved his bulls and could talk bull pedigree for hours. The rest of the meal passed without incident. When dessert was served, Danny gulped his cake, then asked to be excused from the table. Both men visibly relaxed when the boy went into the family room to watch TV.

"How are your folks, Darla?" Daniel asked.

"Dad took up golf and Mom runs around with the Red Hat ladies."

"You tell them I said hello." Daniel pointed his fork at Fletcher. "When do you plan to get us a Christmas tree?"

"I don't know, why?"

"The tree stand on route 37 opens tomorrow. If you wait too long all the good ones will be taken."

"I'm not worried." Fletcher carried an armful of dirty dishes to the sink. When Darla stood to help, he waved her off. "You're company."

She didn't used to be company.

"Fletcher said you're in town for the Keller baptism." Daniel poured coffee into three cups. "Are you staying with your friend?"

Sissy had offered to put Darla up, but her small ranch house was packed with out-of-town relatives, so Darla had declined. "I've got a room at the C'mon Inn." The only motel within a thirty-mile radius of Junket.

"That's no place for a lady. Why don't you stay here? We've got a guest room."

Darla glanced at Fletcher, but he stood at the sink with his back to her. Did he want her to stay? Or go? Seconds ticked by. "Thanks, Daniel, but I'm fine at the motel." She cleared her throat. "I should get going."

"If you change your mind, you're always welcome here." Daniel added cream to his coffee.

Daniel and Fletcher might welcome her, but Danny wouldn't. "Thanks for the lovely meal." She hugged the old man.

"Stop in again before you leave for Dallas." Daniel shuffled from the room.

Fletcher stood by the door. "I'll follow you back to the motel."

"You don't have to."

"I want to."

His husky voice sent shivers down her spine. Darla had no idea where this hometown visit with Fletcher might end up. "Lead the way."

Chapter Three

Fletcher checked the outside temperature reading on the truck's dashboard—52 degrees. Not bad for December. A warm front had stalled over the area the past few days, but the local weatherman predicted that old man winter was barreling their way next week. Maybe Fletcher would suggest a walk once he and Darla arrived at the motel. He wasn't ready to say good-night.

As far as roadside motels went, the C'mon Inn was tacky but he liked the idea that Darla was only fifteen minutes from the ranch. He'd been secretly relieved when she'd insisted on returning to the motel. Even though he'd told Danny that Darla was an old friend, he didn't want to chance upsetting his son by having a strange woman in their home—especially when Danny had been bugging Fletcher to ask Sandi to visit over Christmas break. He hadn't had the heart to tell his son that he'd already extended the invitation, but Sandi had declined, preferring instead to spend the holiday with her bull rider boyfriend.

Up ahead the C'mon Inn's neon green and flamingo-pink sign flashed *Vacancy*. Darla put on her blinker and turned in to the parking lot. Fletcher followed. Holiday lights had been strung around each of the room doors. A blow-up Mrs. and Mr. Claus stood outside the office swaying in the wind. Tinsel had been draped around the office door, which had been sprayed with fake snow.

Was he nuts to wonder if he and Darla could pick things up where they'd left off? Even if by some miracle Darla forgave him for cheating on her in high school when technically they'd been free to see other people, why would she want anything to do with raising another woman's child? Besides, hadn't he decided that a serious relationship was out of the picture until Danny's behavior improved? And lest he forget… *Darla's back in town for a baptism not to rekindle an old flame.*

She pulled the Lexus up to room 17. A sedan with an Enterprise sticker in the back window sat in front of 12 and a late-model Chrysler occupied the space at 9. Fletcher parked in a guest spot and caught up with Darla outside her motel door.

"We didn't have a chance to talk tonight," he said.

"There's a pool around back."

His ego winced. He'd been hoping for an invitation into her room. He nodded to the machine against the building. "Thirsty?"

"Sure." They selected a soda, then entered the motel office. An older man sat behind the check-in desk talking on the phone. A small TV competed with the noisy washer and dryer running in the utility room.

The door on the other side of the lobby led to the pool and hot tub area. Christmas lights had been wrapped around the chain link fence enclosing the patio and green and red lightbulbs had been installed in the hot tub, which

a middle-aged man occupied with a younger woman—
probably a waitress from Larry's Lounge up the road.
Darla weaved through the tables and chairs, picking a
spot in the far corner away from the giggling couple.

"How's your dad coping with your mom's death?"
Darla asked once they were seated.

The last thing he wanted to talk about was his
mother's struggle with cancer. "Better than I anticipated. I think Mom held on longer than she'd wanted to
for Dad's sake." His parents had been deeply in love and
letting go had damn near killed his father. At the time
Fletcher had wondered if he and Sandi would ever come
close to the kind of relationship his mother and father
had shared. He guessed the divorce settled that question.
"A few months ago Dad began seeing a woman from
Midland. He's taken her out to dinner a few times."

"Tell me about Danny." Her expression softened, and
Fletcher sensed her interest was sincere.

"He's having a rough time since Sandi left." Fletcher
sprang from the chair and stood at the fence, staring
into the night.

Darla joined him and her perfume blended with the
smell of damp earth carried on the wind. The heady
aroma made Fletcher want to grasp her hand and drag
her back to room 17 and discover if this grown-up Darla
had any new moves in bed.

"Your dad told me Sandi doesn't spend much time
with him," she said.

Her words abruptly cut off Fletcher's lust-filled
thoughts. A gust of air exploded from his lungs. "All the
boy needs is a little attention from her—a phone call
once in awhile, a letter or package in the mail, a text

message that says she loves him—anything to remind Danny that she hasn't forgotten him."

"I'm sorry." Darla wasn't surprised the woman had walked out on her child. Sandi had been a selfish, stuck-up princess in high school. Her daddy owned the bank in town and she got everything her heart desired, which made Darla wonder what Fletcher ever saw in the shallow woman.

"Shortly after school began Danny's teacher called me in for a conference to discuss his antics in the class-room. Mrs. Tuttle suggested I spend more time with Danny, believing the extra attention would help him adjust to the divorce."

"So what did you do?"

"Each morning I go back to the house after chores and Danny and I eat breakfast together. Instead of making him ride the bus, I drive him to school and pick him up at the end of the day. I help him with his homework in the afternoons. We always eat supper as a family and then I work on the ranch books in my office. When it's bedtime I help Danny get ready and I read to him from one of his *Harry Potter* books." He shook his head. "I'm trying, Darla, but he hasn't responded."

Wanting to comfort Fletcher, Darla squeezed his hand. His fingers tightened around hers and a current of warmth shot up her arm. Like the drop from the top of a roller coaster, memories shot through Darla's mind at high speed. Their first intimate smile. First hug. First hand-holding. First kiss. First…

"I'm worried about how Danny will react when he learns that Sandi has no intention of spending Christ-mas with him."

"Danny and I have a lot in common," Darla said, her eyes following the back-and-forth brush of Fletcher's thumb across her knuckle.

"I grew up with you, Darla Baker. You never acted out in the classroom or gave your parents a hard time."

"No, but I know what it's like to have a mom who ignores you." At his raised eyebrow she explained. "My mom suffered from depression for years and never sought treatment. Not until I was in high school did my father give her an ultimatum—get help or he'd divorce her."

"You never said anything to me about that."

"I didn't want anyone to know. I was ashamed and hurt by her indifference."

"How did you handle it?"

"Not well when I was Danny's age. I didn't understand my mother's illness. I rebelled and sassed her. I wanted her attention even if it was negative attention."

"What did she do when you misbehaved?"

"Instead of spankings or threats she'd sit me down at the kitchen table and use words like shameful, embarrassing and immature to describe my behavior."

"That's rough."

Yes, it was. "Later in life Mom got help and apologized for the way she'd treated me."

"And you're not angry with her anymore?"

"No. We have a much better relationship now. I think it was easy to forgive her because my father had always been there for me. I wasn't totally neglected." Distracted by Fletcher's touch, she pulled her fingers free of his grip. "Be with Danny as much as possible. He'll appreciate the sacrifices you made for him when he's old enough to understand."

Fletcher shoved a hand through his thick, russet hair. Darla recalled running her fingers over the strands when they'd had sex the first time—a stereotypical small-town-up-in-the-hay loft-experience. They'd both ended up with pieces of hay stuck in unmentionable places.

His gaze settled on her face. "Your crummy childhood didn't prevent you from becoming a successful lawyer."

If only she was as successful in her personal life. Her three serious relationships since law school had followed a troubling pattern. Each time her feelings grew serious for her boyfriend and he moved in with her, suddenly she found herself watching the clock and timing his arrival home from work. When he or she traveled on business she texted him or called him on his cell to find out where he was, who he was with and what he was doing. In the end she'd broken off the engagement because she hadn't been able to trust him not to cheat on her.

Fletcher's heavy-lidded gaze chipped away at Darla's determination to put this man out of her mind and heart for good.

"We've been dancing around the subject since you arrived," he said.

Darla knew exactly what *subject* he referred to— Amy Frazer.

Resting his arms across the top of the fence, he said, "This is tougher than I thought it would be."

All of a sudden, Darla wasn't sure discussing the past was the answer to moving on. Why open up old wounds? Maybe it was best to admit mistakes were made on both sides and that it was time to forgive and forget.

Can you forgive?

She had no choice if she wanted to put the past behind her. "We've both done things we regret." If she'd given him a chance to explain his actions in high school, who knows, they might have made amends and contin-ued dating through college and beyond. But that's not what happened and there was no going back for either of them. She wasn't the same Darla anymore. She had a career and had made a life for herself far away from Junket. "I'm leaving in a couple of days and—"

"You owe me a chance to explain, Darla."

She didn't *owe* him anything. "What if I'm not ready to hear your explanation?"

"Then stay until you are." He inched closer—within touching distance, but kept his hands to himself. The fact that Darla wished he'd pull her into his arms proved how chaotic her feelings for him were.

"Come with Danny and me tomorrow to pick out a Christmas tree."

She doubted Danny would appreciate her tagging along on their tree-scouting trip, but there was a vul-nerability in Danny that reached inside Darla and tugged on her heartstrings. And spending more time with Fletcher might prove her feelings for him were nothing more than nostalgic memories. "All right. Count me in tomorrow."

"I LIKE THIS ONE!" Danny raced across the tree lot and pointed to a giant blue spruce. "No, this one's better!" He bolted two rows over and tugged on the branch of another tree.

The child zigzagged through the trees until Darla's eyes threatened to cross. She noticed the muscle along Fletcher's jaw bunch. *Dad* was losing his patience.

"Why don't you ask about the prices of the trees while I help Danny look around?"

Relief flashed across Fletcher's face. "Are you sure?"

She suspected he hesitated to leave her alone with Danny because the boy had been rude to her a short time ago when they'd picked her up at the motel. The pout on Danny's face had been a dead giveaway that he resented her presence.

"We'll be fine." As soon as Fletcher walked off she spotted a flash of blue—Danny's jacket. She headed in that direction. "Look at this one." She stopped a few feet away. Danny peeked at her through the tree branches. "I'm wondering if it's too tall for your living room."

Danny gave up his hiding place and joined her. He shifted from one foot to the other—his mind studying the tree, his body urging him to run. "This is the first tree you pointed to when we arrived."

He crinkled his nose at her.

"Then you ran to this one." She walked a few feet away and motioned to a smaller tree. "It's short and round. Another good choice."

"It is?"

"Sure. There's room for lots of ornaments."

"We don't got lots of ornaments."

"I could show you and your dad how to make Christmas ornaments out of dough."

Danny scowled. "We don't need your help."

She ignored his rudeness and pointed to a medium-sized tree.

"I didn't pick that one," Danny said.

"Hmm. I could have sworn you ran past this tree. It's perfect."

He scuffed his shoe against the ground. "Maybe I did."

"It's tall, but not too tall. Round, but not too round. What do you think? You're the expert."

Danny pretended to study the tree with a critical eye. "I guess it's okay. Do you think Dad will like it?"

"I don't see why not."

"Hey, you two. Made a decision?"

Darla motioned to the evergreen behind them. "Danny's got an eye for trees. He picked the best one on the lot." The boy's face lit up at her compliment.

Fletcher circled the tree, studying all sides. "Good job, Danny." His cell phone rang, but he ignored it. "I'll go pay for it."

"Your grandfather will love this tree," Darla said when she and Danny were alone.

"I guess."

"Something the matter?"

"My mom hated our tree last year."

"Not everyone gets in the holiday spirit, Danny." Darla's mother had never made a big deal out of Christmas. Most holidays her mom hid in the bedroom and refused to come out. "Let's wait for your dad at the truck." Danny kept himself amused playing with a bungee cord until Fletcher arrived with the tree. Once the evergreen had been tied down, they left the lot.

"Since Danny picked out such a nice tree we should celebrate and eat out for lunch," Darla said.

"Yeah!" Danny bounced on the backseat.

"Where do you want—"

"Crusty's!" Danny interrupted Darla.

Fletcher grinned. "Pizza's his favorite."

Crusty's was crowded, but Darla didn't run into

anyone from her past. A waitress seated them in a booth and took their order. As soon as she walked off, Fletcher emptied his pockets of change and Danny scooped up the coins, then sprinted to the arcade. Fletcher expelled a deep breath and flashed a sexy half grin.

His smile reminded her that for a short while today she'd forgotten the past and had lived in the moment with Fletcher and Danny. Shaken by the realization, she shored up her defenses and reminded herself that the goal of spending time with Fletcher wasn't about second chances, but about moving on. Sooner or later the cowboy would say or do something that proved they weren't meant for a happy-ever-after.

"Thanks for coming with us today." He grasped her hand. "I'm sorry Danny treated you rudely earlier this morning."

Darla didn't have an opportunity to tell him it was no big deal, because Danny reappeared at their booth. She pulled her hand free of Fletcher's grip. No sense upsetting the child needlessly.

"I suck at Night Raider," the boy said, sliding onto the seat next to his father.

"We don't use that kind of language, son."

"Grandpa says God damn and he doesn't get in trouble."

Darla sipped her soda to keep from laughing.

"That's enough, Danny."

"Sorry," he muttered, then slurped his drink.

"What are your plans tomorrow after the baptism?" Fletcher asked.

"Sissy's having a cookout."

"How long do you have to stay?"

She'd been hoping to make an appearance and then leave after an hour. "I should be able to get away early in the afternoon. Why?"

"Spend the rest of the day with us," Fletcher said.

Darla's gaze cut to Danny, but the boy was busy scribbling on the paper table-covering with crayons the waitress had supplied. "I'm not sure—"

"I am." Fletcher grinned.

She doubted Danny wanted to see her again. Would the boy's attitude change toward her if she showed him a little extra attention? "We could make ornaments for the tree."

The crayon in Danny's hand froze. "I don't want to make ornaments," he said.

"Making ornaments could be a lot of fun." Fletcher's comment didn't erase the boy's scowl.

"Ms. Baker and I will find something else to do if you don't want to make decorations," Fletcher said.

"I guess it's okay," Danny muttered.

Just as Darla suspected—Danny didn't want her to be alone with his father. Maybe she should respect Danny's wishes, because what if spending more time with Fletcher backfired and, instead of getting over him, she fell more under his spell?

Chapter Four

"Mornin'," greeted Darla when she stepped out of her motel room Sunday and found Fletcher leaning against the hood of his truck.

"What are you doing here?"

"Thought I'd give you a ride to church." His eyes roamed over her cream ruffled blouse and navy skirt.

She took in Fletcher's dress slacks, brown sport coat and his Sunday-go-to-meeting boots. "You're going to church, too?"

"Every Sunday, darlin'." His green eyes twinkled.

Sure. "Where's Danny?" She shielded her eyes against the early morning sun but couldn't see if the boy sat inside the vehicle.

"Dad's taking him to Sunday school." He held open the passenger-side door for her.

She supposed it wouldn't hurt to ride with him to the church. She could catch a lift to the baptism party with one of Sissy's relatives. As soon as she clicked her seat belt she wondered if she was crazy being seen with her old flame in public. Tongues would wag.

Fletcher drove toward Junket. "Nervous?"

The cowboy always did know when her insides were tied in knots. "No." She waved a hand in the air and the motion stirred the scent of a familiar cologne. "You're wearing the same cologne I bought you in high school."

"I like the smell."

That's it? He wore the scent for years because he liked the smell?

"And it reminds me of you."

A surge of pleasure rushed through Darla, but she caught herself before she returned Fletcher's smile. A long time ago the naïve Darla would have fallen for his flattery, but the more worldly Darla didn't trust words. Actions counted more.

Conversation stalled for a few minutes while they listened to talk radio on the way into town. Darla shifted on the seat for the umpteenth time, worried about running into people she hadn't seen in years.

"What's wrong?"

"Nothing, why?"

"The way you're squirming I figured I'd accidentally flipped the bun warmer switch and your fanny was roasting."

"Funny." Darla rolled her eyes. She'd missed Fletcher's teasing. "I'm concerned I won't remember names." Half truth. Mostly she feared people asking personal questions about her life. Once they learned she was single at the age of thirty they'd jump to the conclusion that she'd pined for Fletcher all these years.

"I'll help you with the names," Fletcher said. "A few new families in town attend church, but you'll recognize everyone else."

The parking lot was crowded—probably due to the

Keller baptism. The tension in Darla inched upward. *Just get through today and then you'll be on your way back to Dallas. Back to your condo. Back to your job. Your coworkers.*

Your lonely life.

She recognized three of the four couples entering the building ahead of her and Fletcher. Darla took comfort in the warm press of Fletcher's hand against the small of her back as they ascended the church steps. Once inside the sanctuary she pulled away, not wishing to give the parishioners the idea they were a couple again.

Sissy caught her attention and motioned to a pew up front. "I need to sit near the Kellers," Darla said.

"Lead the way." She slid into the third pew, then swallowed a groan when she discovered Mr. and Mrs. Abernathy a few feet away. What rotten luck she picked seats next to her mother's childhood friend.

Gladys smiled. "How wonderful to see you, Darla."

"You're looking well, Mrs. Abernathy."

The church organist introduced the first hymn and the congregation stood to sing. Fletcher's father joined them in the pew and after the song ended the minister recited a prayer and the congregation sat. Halfway through the service Sunday school classes were released and the school-aged children flooded the sanctuary, making lots of noise as they searched for their families. Instead of sitting at the end of the pew next to his grandfather, Danny squished between Fletcher and Darla. Good. She needed the boy to remind her that there were plenty of valid reasons to resist the temptation to forget the past and start over with Fletcher.

At the end of the service Pastor Ferguson announced the baptism of Emma Keller and asked the child's parents and godparents to join him before the congregation. Little Emma slept through the entire ceremony— not even the cold water droplets the pastor dabbed on her forehead disturbed her. After the prayer, the congregation sang a final hymn, then Pastor Ferguson stood outside on the church steps, shaking hands with the parishioners as they headed to the parking lot.

"You didn't tell me you were coming to church with Fletcher," Sissy whispered.

"It's no big deal." Darla's gaze narrowed on Fletcher who conversed with a man she didn't recognize.

Sissy handed Emma to her mother-in-law. "What's going on between you two?"

"Nothing."

"If it's nothing then why can't you take your eyes off him?" Sissy asked.

Good grief. Darla forced her attention from Fletcher and focused on her friend. "It's complicated."

"I'm listening."

Darla sighed. "I thought spending time with Fletcher would prove that I'm over him. That we're different people. That I can finally let go of the past."

"But?"

She shrugged. "He still makes me feel things."

"You're not in lo—"

"No." Darla was not in love with Fletcher McFadden. *Who are you trying to convince—Sissy or you?* "Whatever feelings I have for him are part of my past. Besides, it could never work out between us."

"Why not?"

"For obvious reasons. I have a career and a life in Dallas. I'm not giving that up."

"We'll talk about this later." Sissy grasped her arm. "I meant to tell you earlier but you arrived too late with Fletcher. Emma's running a low-grade temperature."

"Nothing serious I hope."

"She's teething. I'm delaying the party and cookout until early this evening. I want Emma to take a nap and frankly I need one after being up all night with her."

"That's fine. What time should I drop over?"

"We'll fire up the grill between five and six." Sissy glanced at Fletcher. "I imagine you'll find something to do until then…?"

Fletcher watched Darla hug her friend, but when Sissy walked off with her family, Darla remained behind. "Aren't you heading to the baptism party?" he asked, when she joined him at the church doors.

"Little Emma's not feeling well, so the barbecue's been delayed until tonight."

"What's wrong with the baby?" he asked.

"Sissy says she's teething."

His face broke out in a wide smile. "That means we can have lunch before you show Danny and I how to make Christmas decorations."

Drat. She'd forgotten about the promise she'd made yesterday. "I guess that would be fine."

"Great." He escorted her out of the building, then Darla excused herself to say hello to Mrs. Franks who waved from beneath the big oak near the parking lot.

Danny and Fletcher's father stood on the sidewalk waiting for Fletcher. "Where are we gonna eat?" Danny asked, tugging on Fletcher's sport coat pocket. The traditional Sunday pot-roast meal had passed away along with Fletcher's mother. He and his father had begun a new tradition—eating Sunday brunch out.

"It's up to Grandpa, Danny. I'm taking Ms. Baker to lunch."

"We'll scrounge up something at home," his father said. He patted Danny's shoulder but the boy shrugged off the touch.

"I wanna go with you," Danny whined.

"Ms. Baker and I won't be long. We're making Christmas decorations this afternoon, remember?"

"I don't want to make any dumb decorations." Danny stomped off toward his grandfather's truck.

"He'll get over it," his father said, then followed Danny to the parking lot.

Fletcher wished he knew the words to reassure his son that he didn't have to feel threatened by Darla. He admitted there were days he missed the intimacies between a woman and a man. His relationship with Sandi had never been like that. He'd never been able to read her mind. Or finish her sentences. Or know what she wanted before she asked for it. He'd had that kind of relationship with Darla once.

But you blew it.

There was no going back for him and Darla. And no going forward—not until Danny conquered his insecurities over his mother's abandonment. The boy couldn't make it any clearer that he didn't want his father involved with another woman. For now Fletcher intended to enjoy what little time he had with Darla.

Easier said than done, because right now. Right here. He wanted more from her than a little time.

FLETCHER CUT ACROSS the front lawn and stopped a re-
spectable distance from the chatting women and waited
for one of them to notice him. Neither did, which left
him no choice but to eavesdrop. He wished he hadn't.

"Your parents must be so proud of you, Darla," Mrs.
Franks said. "Traveling to China—imagine that."

China?

"Visiting the Great Wall was an incredible experience. If I hadn't needed to return to Dallas for a trial I
would have extended the business trip another week."

"Where else have you visited?" Mrs. Franks asked.

"Ireland, but that was for pleasure, not business."

Pleasure—as in pleasure with a guy?

Feminine voices droned on and Fletcher's thoughts
drifted in another direction. Up until this moment, he'd
acknowledged that Darla had lived a vastly different life
from him but he'd always believed they had a lot in
common. They'd grown up in Junket, knew the same
people, went to the same church, same schools, same
birthday parties. But all that had ended with their high
school graduation.

The worldly Darla fascinated him, but did down-
home Fletcher interest *her* anymore? He possessed a
college degree but remained a small-town guy at heart.
Was there any small-town girl left in Darla?

There he went again…worrying about how the years
had changed them, when he needed to steer clear of a
serious relationship for the time being. And if what
Darla had said was true—that she'd come close to
marrying a few times—then she probably wasn't ready
to settle down either.

"Excuse me, ladies." Both women jumped. He nodded to Mrs. Franks, before making eye contact with Darla. "We'll be late for lunch if we don't head out now."

Mrs. Franks glanced between Darla and Fletcher. "I didn't realize you two were dating."

"We're just—"

"Friends," Fletcher interrupted.

"I see." The older woman hugged Darla. "I enjoyed our chat. Tell your folks I said hello." Mrs. Franks joined the other gossipmongers gathering on the front lawn.

Uncaring that his actions might provoke more gossip, he grasped Darla's hand and led the way to his truck. When she didn't tug her hand free, he tightened his grip.

"Where are we going?" she asked.

"You'll see." He intended to take her to Connie's Coney Dogs on highway 51—their favorite high-school-date-night hangout.

Ten minutes later when Fletcher pulled into the gravel lot in front of the hot dog stand, Darla said, "It's been years since I've had a Coney dog." She laughed. "Remember when you and Logan had a hot-dog-eating contest the day of the homecoming football game?"

"Yeah, I was sicker than a *dog* during the game."

She grinned at his lame joke. "No wonder—you ate twelve chili dogs."

"I won you that crown, didn't I?" He hesitated before asking, "What did you ever do with that thing?" The headpiece consisted of plastic hot dogs glued end-to-end to form a circle.

"It's packed away in a box somewhere."

"Really?"

"You act surprised."

"I thought…well…since…" He shrugged.

"I have the single daisy you gave me in the second grade pressed between the pages of my favorite Sweet Valley High book." A sigh that sounded as if it had been suppressed for months, maybe years squeezed past her lips. "I saved the poem you wrote for me in tenth grade. The heart-shaped locket you bought me for my six-teenth birthday."

"Darla, I'm—"

"Starving. Let's order lunch." She hopped out of the truck and slammed the door, effectively ending his attempt to apologize for his past sins.

Darla's confession left Fletcher light-headed as if he'd downed a six-pack, one beer after the other. Was it possible that a little piece of him had remained in Darla's heart all these years? She must feel something for him if she hadn't been able to bring herself to toss out his gifts.

He joined her at the stand and they placed their orders, then took the food to a picnic table beneath the shade of a large bur oak.

"Mmm. As good as I remembered," Darla said.

Fletcher was too caught up in watching her chew to comment.

"What's the matter?" she asked.

"Bee. Hold still." He brushed the imaginary insect from her neck, his fingers making contact with her skin. She sucked in a quiet breath. There it was—the rush…the heat they felt when they touched. Twelve years and other lovers had done nothing to curb the attraction between them.

Why did Darla have to drop into his life and tempt

him to throw caution to the wind and start over with her?
"I'm sorry."

Her gaze shifted to the half-eaten hot dog in her hands.

"I know that *sorry* doesn't change the past. Or make
you feel better. Or make me any less of a jerk for what
I did. But please believe me when I say that I didn't set
out to hurt you on purpose."

Her watery gaze sucker punched him in the gut. "I
don't know why I'm crying." She sniffed. "Good grief,
that was another lifetime ago."

"I wish it were yesterday."

"Why?"

"I would never have taken Amy Frazer to the drive-
in movies. But I was mad at you for deciding that we
needed to take a break from each other."

Darla's mouth opened, then closed without making
a sound.

"No matter what others might have said, I didn't
sleep with Amy."

"Sissy claimed the windows were steamed."

Fletcher grinned. "I never said we didn't get a little
carried away." Then he sobered. "I wanted to make you
jealous so you'd agree to go out with me again. I didn't
expect you to quit speaking to me in the hallways or stop
taking my calls."

"I forgive you." Her smile was tinged with sadness.
"We were young and stupid."

"I have another confession to make," he said. "I
never stopped thinking about you, even while I was
married to Sandi."

The urge to get up from the table and flee caught
Darla by surprise and she forced herself to remain

seated. She gazed into Fletcher's green eyes and the honesty in them stole her breath. She wasn't the only one who needed closure.

"I kept the love letters you wrote me in high school. Sandi found them shortly after Danny was born. Those letters were her excuse for having the affair." He fisted his hands. "She said I was just as guilty of cheating as she was."

Fletcher had kept her letters. Darla's throat ached with sadness. "How did you and Sandi end up together?"

"I ran into her at a bar in Midland. I was up there on business and stopped to have a beer before heading home." He shook his head. "After a few drinks we left the bar and ended up in a motel room off the interstate."

"Are you telling me Danny's the result of a one-night stand?"

"Yep."

All these years, Darla believed Fletcher had dated Sandi before they'd gotten married.

"The next morning Sandi and I agreed to forget about what we did and go our separate ways. Two months later she called me with the news she was pregnant." He stared off into space. "There was nothing left to do but get married."

"If you didn't love each other why get married?" Today there was little stigma attached to single women having babies out of wedlock.

"Because I was Danny's father and no child of mine was coming into this world without my name on the birth certificate."

That was the Fletcher she knew—old-fashioned and responsible.

Learning the particulars of Fletcher's involvement with Sandi satisfied her curiosity but the truth was bittersweet. For years she'd pined for a man who'd been married to a woman he'd never loved. Created a family with that woman—a family that by all rights should have been hers.

Maybe the temptation to try again with Fletcher was so strong and so real because she'd always wondered what would have happened to them if they'd kissed and made up. Maybe it was the not knowing that had led to her commitment issues with other men.

Right now she didn't want to think about second chances, the past or the future. She checked her watch. "We should get back to your place. Danny probably wonders where we are."

The drive to the Rocking J was made in silence.

"I THOUGHT Dad was supposed to make ornaments," groused Danny.

"I'm sure he'll be back soon," Darla said.

When she and Fletcher arrived at the ranch, Fletcher and his father had been called to the breeding barn for an emergency, leaving Darla to entertain Danny. She'd suggested preparing the dough for the ornament making while they waited for his father to return but Danny snubbed his nose at her idea and had left the kitchen.

Undeterred, Darla went to work, banging pots and pans, hoping to entice the little rascal back into the kitchen. Her plan worked. Danny hovered in the doorway, wearing his usual scowl, but his eyes followed her movements around the room.

"Danny, where did your mother store the measuring cups?"

For a moment she thought the boy wouldn't answer, then he opened a drawer near the sink. "Right there."

"Thanks." She motioned to the bag of flour on the counter. "I could use your help so I don't spill on my clothes."

He hesitated, then said, "Okay."

Darla pulled a chair next to the counter and Danny climbed onto the seat. "Measure out two cups of flour and pour it into this bowl." After he did as instructed, she said, "Now we need one cup of table salt."

Danny hopped off the chair and grabbed the salt shaker from the middle of the kitchen table.

"We'll need more than that." She opened and closed cupboards until she found the salt container. "Use this." Danny spilled extra on the counter and glanced at her. "Don't worry. We'll clean up later."

"What's next?" he asked.

"One cup of water." After he poured the water into the bowl she said, "The last thing we need is a tablespoon of vegetable oil to help make the dough easier to work with." The bottle of oil was full so she poured while Danny held the tablespoon over the bowl. "Good. Now stir." She handed him a fork.

While Danny struggled to blend the ingredients, Darla put away the flour, oil and salt. "Once you have the dough mixed we'll add food coloring to make it look Christmasy."

"Who cares about Christmas?" Danny muttered.

Compassion filled Darla and she yearned to reach out to the boy but she had no experience with children. Maybe all he needed was for someone to listen to him. "Sounds like Christmas isn't your favorite holiday."

He shook his head. "It sucks."

She ignored the foul language. "Why's that?"

"'Cause I won't get what I want."

"Oh? What do you want?"

"My mom back."

"It must be hard not having your mom here everyday."

He nodded. "Dad says Mom's really busy and has to travel all the time, but he's lying."

"Why would your father lie?"

"Because my mom doesn't love me anymore." Danny's voice cracked and without thinking Darla hugged the child close, brushing his blond locks from his forehead.

"Your mother loves you, Danny, she—"

"No, she doesn't." He wiggled out of her hold. "You're just saying that."

"I know she loves you and I'll tell you how I know." Darla sat at the kitchen table and motioned for Danny to join her. "I grew up with a mother who was always home but never there for me."

"Huh?"

"My mother suffered from an illness called depression. When I was little she'd ignore me or lock herself in her bedroom all day and sleep."

"Why?"

"My mother didn't do it on purpose. The illness caused her to shut herself off from me and my father. But when I was a little girl I thought my mother didn't love me. Once I got older and understood more about her illness I realized she loved me the best way she could under the circumstances."

"Does my mom have an illness, too?"

Maybe she shouldn't have used her own mother as an example. "I don't think so, Danny. But some people aren't able to show their love for us like we wish them to." Then she asked, "If you could change your mom how would you want her to show she loves you?"

His slim shoulders shrugged. "I would make her live with me. And come watch me play soccer. And cook me breakfast. And hug me."

"I bet it's tough to go without those things." Darla patted his arm. This time Danny didn't pull away.

"My dad hugs me a lot and he goes to my soccer games."

"You're lucky to have a father who loves you so much."

"And a grandpa."

"That's right. Your grandpa loves you a whole bunch, too."

"Can I make my dad something for Christmas?"

Danny's question effectively ended the absentee-mom discussion. "You bet. How about a decoration your dad can put on the desk in his office and see everyday?"

"Like a snowman?"

"That's a great idea." Darla sectioned off a piece of white dough for Danny to roll into three different size balls. She separated the rest of the dough into two containers, then added red and green food coloring. "You can make a red scarf and a green hat for your snowman."

While Danny worked on his project, Darla rolled out the remaining dough and used the cookie cutters she'd found in the pantry to make several Christmas trees, angels and stars. Once those were lined up on a baking sheet, she took the tip of a pencil eraser and poked a hole through the top to make room for a ribbon or tree hook.

"Ready?" Darla asked when the oven finished pre-heating.

"How does it look?" Danny held up his lopsided snowman.

"He's terrific. I like how long you made the scarf. Once it's baked and cooled off you can paint the face."

"What's going on in here?" Daniel McFadden waltzed into the kitchen.

"I'm making Dad's Christmas present." Danny pointed to the object. "Guess what it is."

Daniel examined the gift with great care. "I'd say this is best-looking snowman I've ever seen." He ruffled his grandson's hair.

"Do you think Dad's gonna like it?" Danny set the snowman on the baking sheet.

"Don't see why not." Daniel's gaze shifted around the messy kitchen. "Looks like you two have been busy."

Darla slid the baking sheet into the oven. "Making a few tree decorations."

Danny carried the dirty bowl and utensils to the sink. "Can I go outside and play on the swings, Grandpa?"

"Sure." Once the back door slammed shut Daniel said, "You and Danny appear to be getting along."

"He misses his mother."

Daniel sat at the table while Darla washed dishes. "Has Fletcher talked about his divorce?"

"A bit," she hedged.

"He and Sandi should never have married."

Startled by the comment, Darla scrubbed the dried salt off the cooking utensils and waited for Daniel to continue.

"I don't approve of babies being born out of wedlock and I certainly expected my son to stand up and take re-

sponsibility for his actions, but it didn't take a genius to
see those two were like oil and water."

But Fletcher was an honorable man and felt a duty
to marry.

"Sandi refused to marry at first."

Refused?

"Her father forced her into the marriage. Benjamin
worried that the scandal would ruin his banking business." Daniel shook his head. "The ass. He only cared
about his business, not what was best for his daughter
or my son."

Darla imagined the couple's wedding was a solemn
affair. Then the honeymoon…she closed the door on
that thought.

"I always thought you and Fletcher would tie the
knot one day."

"Really?"

"Back when you two dated in high school Fletcher
asked me when I knew for sure I wanted to marry his
mother. We talked some about relationships, love and
marriage. I told him he could have the land out by the
pond to build a house for himself and his bride one day."

How many nights had she and Fletcher sat on a
blanket and studied the stars by that pond? They'd
shared hundred of wishes and dreams with each other.

"Sandi refused to live at the ranch." He shook his
head. "She didn't take to motherhood and left most of the
child-rearing up to Fletcher, day cares and preschools.
When Sandi would take off for days at a time Marilyn
would drive up to Midland and help out, but then she got
sick and Fletcher was on his own with Danny."

That Fletcher's marriage was anything but a fairy

tale gave Darla little comfort. The news made her sad. Sad for Danny, who'd been shamelessly neglected by his mother. Sad for Sandi, who'd thrown the gift of motherhood aside and had put herself first. Sad for Fletcher whose one bad decision had cost him dearly. Sad for herself—a woman who was still searching for her Prince Charming among all the toads.

"To tell the truth I was damned glad Fletcher caught Sandi cheating," Daniel said. "Gave him an excuse to send the woman packing."

"Were Sandi's parents upset?"

"They didn't blame Fletcher once Sandi confessed she'd been sneaking off with that bull rider her entire marriage."

Good Lord, that must have devastated Fletcher. And changed him.

"I've always liked you, Darla. You've been a daughter to me since the day you showed up at the door with a bloody knee, accusing Fletcher of pushing you down, so he could be the first one on the school bus."

"I pushed him first." She shared a grin with Daniel.

"Who pushed who?" Fletcher entered the kitchen, his glance bouncing between his father and Darla.

Darla popped off her chair and checked the dough in the oven. "I pushed you the first day of kindergarten so I could get on the bus before you."

"That's not the way I remembered it," Fletcher said.

"Oh?"

"I *let* you push me." He grinned.

Darla glanced at the kitchen clock. "I need to return to the motel and freshen up before the barbecue at Sissy's."

"But you just got here."

Two hours ago.

"When are you leaving town?" Daniel asked.

"Tomorrow morning." She hugged the older man. "I'm glad we had a chance to visit." She pointed to the oven. "The dough will be done in a half hour."

"I'll keep an eye on it." Daniel paused in the doorway. "Don't stay away so long next time."

Darla faced Fletcher. "Ready?" She needed time alone to try and make sense of all the feelings running amuck inside her.

Chapter Five

"Stay," Fletcher said outside Darla's motel room.

He crowded her space—his scent swirling around her, making it difficult to breathe let alone think. Before Darla realized his intent, Fletcher's mouth captured hers. His lips caressed, cajoled and teased.

His tongue worked magic and the warmth in her stomach radiated upward engulfing her breasts. No man had ever sparked a fire this hot inside her with just a kiss.

A groan rumbled in his chest and she pressed her hand to his thundering heart. He cupped her face, his fingers sifting through her hair—making a mess of her carefully styled locks. Aware of the danger he posed to her heart, Darla attempted to mentally retreat but Fletcher's kiss made it impossible.

If they hadn't been standing out in the open she was certain he'd have laid her down on the sidewalk and made love to her. Even more troubling… She wouldn't have stopped him. The realization shocked her like a bucket of icy water over the head. She broke off the kiss.

Face ruddy with passion, Fletcher's ragged breathing and glowing eyes exposed his aroused state. How often had she seen that face in her dreams? She accepted the fact that they were sexually attracted to one another. The chemistry between them had always been powerful, combustible and exciting.

"Talk to me," he said. "What are you thinking?"

That I should run.

He smoothed his finger across her lip, drawing a shiver from her body. "If it's possible I want you even more now than I did in high school."

She wanted him, too. And he knew it. "Sex will complicate things." She would have increased the space between them, but her traitorous feet had bonded to the pavement. "My life, my job, my friends are in Dallas." *But there's no lover.*

When Fletcher remained silent she added, "Your dad's getting up there in years. Pretty soon you'll take over the entire bull-breeding operation. Danny's school and his friends are in Junket. And Danny's having a difficult time with Sandi's absence."

"I've already taken those things into account, Darla. I'm not asking for forever."

Pain squeezed her rib cage. What exactly was he asking for? A fling? An affair? A one-night stand?

Feeling the walls close in on her, she said, "I can't stay. I'm due in court on Tuesday."

"Then come back after the trial."

Where was the offer to visit her in Dallas? Why did she have to make all the concessions? "I need time to think things through."

His eyes narrowed and she expected him to argue with her. Instead, he said, "When you're contemplating…think about this." His gaze zeroed in on her mouth.

Oh, no. Not again.

This kiss wasn't a peck on the cheek or a quick brush against her lips. His mouth covered hers, open and wet. Fletcher didn't know how to kiss any other way but all-out.

The kiss ended too soon. "I'll be here when you make up your mind."

Darla watched his truck leave the parking lot, wondering who would give in first—her or Fletcher.

"Ms. BAKER." The law firm's secretary buzzed the intercom on Darla's phone Friday morning. "A Mr. Fletcher McFadden is on line two."

Fletcher? Four days had passed since they'd said goodbye at the C'mon Inn. After returning to Dallas on Monday, she'd dialed his number several times but hung up before the call had connected. And each night after work she'd checked the caller ID on the home phone hoping his number would show up. It hadn't.

"Hello, Fletcher."

"I'm sorry to bother you at work, Darla, but something's come up and I need…I need you."

Her heart soared.

"It concerns Danny."

Danny? He needed her for his son? Her heart nosedived back to earth. "What happened?"

"Danny's been expelled from school until after Christmas break."

"What did he do?"

"He freed the ferret from its cage in the science lab. The kids went crazy chasing the thing around and all hell broke loose. By the time the dust settled, the lab was in shambles and two of the students had been cut by broken glass. The principal's sending me the bill."

"I'm sure Danny didn't intend for anyone to get hurt."

"No, he didn't." Fletcher's groan reached through the connection and tugged on her heartstrings. "Darla, Danny hasn't stopped talking about you since you left Sunday afternoon."

Danny missed her?

"I asked him why he broke the rules in the science lab but he refuses to tell me. Would you drive down here this weekend and speak with him?"

"What makes you think he'll tell *me* the truth?"

"Because he said he would."

"He did?" Darla smelled a setup.

"I don't know what the two of you discussed the afternoon you made Christmas decorations, but Danny hasn't been the same since you left. He needs you, Darla."

How in the world did she say no to a little boy who was suffering from his mother's neglect?

Did she dare return to Junket and risk becoming closer to Danny? And what about Fletcher? Would they be able to keep a lid on their sexual attraction to one another? The fact that her desire for the cowboy burned hotter than ever, despite his having broken her high-school heart was disconcerting. What if she and Fletcher crossed the line? Then what?

Danny's needs take precedence over yours.

"I have several vacation days left this year," she hedged. "I suppose I could stay for a few days…until Danny's—"

"Great. I knew I could count on you."

Now if only she could count on her heart not to betray her with Fletcher.

"We'll get the guest bedroom ready."

A mini panic attack erupted inside Darla. Living in close quarters with Fletcher would tax her defenses, but residing at the C'mon Inn made little sense if she intended to help his son. "I'll see you Saturday afternoon."

"We'll be waiting."

Darla wondered what other surprises awaited her at the Rocking J.

DARLA HAD BEEN at the Rocking J three days and Danny had yet to confide in her why he opened the ferret's cage at school. Each time she broached the topic he changed the subject. She found it interesting that when she and Danny first met he'd instantly disliked her and now they palled around like best friends. Something was up in that little brain of his and she was determined to figure out what.

That afternoon they sat on the rug in the living room near the Christmas tree playing the board game Battleship. Daniel was busy in the kitchen baking a cake and Fletcher had left over an hour ago to meet the vet to check on a bull.

"You know what I think?" she said, studying the rows of ships in front of her.

"Huh?"

"I think you opened the ferret's cage at school because you were hoping that getting into trouble would make your mother come home."

Danny's brown eyes widened.

Bingo!

His gaze dropped to the game board. "That's sorta why."

"Sorta?"

After a minute, he peeked at Darla. "I wanted you to come back here."

Darla's heart burst wide open. "Why?"

"Because I need you to help me make my mom come home."

Pain, sharp and blunt stabbed her blooming heart until it wilted and collapsed upon itself. Danny didn't want her—he wanted her help in convincing Sandi to change her mind about being with him.

"I know Dad's really mad 'cause I got kicked out of school but if Mom comes back, then we can be happy again."

"Danny, I don't know how to help you." Darla needed to speak with Fletcher as soon as possible. Someone had to sit down with this child and explain that Sandi wasn't going to be a part of the family anymore.

"Dad says we're gonna go to the rodeo and Mom's gonna be there. I wanna buy her a special Christmas gift that'll make her miss me."

Darla's eyes burned but she refused to allow her tears to fall in front of the boy. "And you want me to help you pick out a gift for your mother?"

"Yeah, 'cause Dad can't know. I wanna surprise him, too."

She supposed she'd have to pay for this *gift*. Not that she cared. What mattered was Danny and the possibility that his plan might not work. How would the boy handle another rejection by his mother?

Or worse…What if Danny's gift makes Sandi realize

she's got her priorities screwed up and she wants to rec-
oncile with Fletcher?

Damned if she did. Damned if she didn't. "When do
you want to go shopping, Danny?"

"How's the bull?" his father asked when Fletcher
walked in the house late Monday afternoon.

The prize-winning bull had cut himself on a splin-
tered fence post and the wound had been slow to heal.
"Better. Vet took out the stitches."

Fletcher's eyes strayed to Darla, who stood at the
stove stirring a pot of boiling noodles. She looked
pretty today—more like a country girl. Her hair wasn't
styled and sprayed into place, but the soft locks fell
every which way, resembling a fairy-tale pixie. Her
outfit—jeans and a sweatshirt—reminded him of all
the Saturdays they'd hung out at her parents' drugstore
after he finished his chores for the day. He'd helped
her father in the stockroom and Darla had tended the
soda fountain.

"Dad," Fletcher said. "Mind watching Danny for
the rest of the day?" With his son and his father
around, finding alone time with Darla had been impossible. Sitting across from her at the supper table,
smelling her perfume throughout the house and not
being able to touch her was driving him nuts. He'd
awoken this morning with a plan guaranteed to land
him a kiss by day's end. Maybe more if he played his
cards right.

"Sure, I'll watch Danny," his father said. "You got
plans?"

"Darla and I are going for a ride." Ignoring his

father's surprised expression, he smiled at Darla, daring her to object.

"What about supper?" she asked.

His father waved her off. "Don't worry. You two can eat the leftovers tomorrow."

"Give me five minutes."

As soon as he heard Darla's footsteps climb the stairs to the second floor, he asked, "Is Danny behaving?"

"That boy minds around Darla. How about yourself?"

"What do you mean?"

"You plan to behave around her, too?" His father's eyebrow arched.

"Not if I can help it."

"That's my boy." He patted Fletcher on the shoulder, then lifted the pot from the burner and dumped the noodles into the colander in the sink.

Fletcher hoped his surprise wouldn't backfire. He intended to show Darla that Danny wasn't the only McFadden male who needed her. His cell phone went off. Logan again. Damn, he'd forgotten to check in with his friend. Too late now.

Darla returned to the kitchen, waved to his father and followed Fletcher out to the utility porch. He lifted an old sheepskin coat from a hook on the wall. "Use this."

"What's wrong with my jacket?" She slipped off the white ski coat.

"Looks goofy." He held the sheepskin out and she thrust her arms into the sleeves.

"If you're trying to woo me with words like *goofy,* you won't get far."

Words were the last thing he intended to woo her

with. He nuzzled the soft patch of skin below her ear where she was ticklish. "Mmm. You smell good."

She giggled, then squirmed from his arms. "Where are we going?"

"You'll see." He ushered her outside.

"We're riding in that?" She gaped at the horse-drawn buckboard.

"Hop up." He planted his hand against her fanny as she climbed onto the bench seat.

"Watch it, buster," she mumbled.

"Yes, ma'am." He tipped his hat.

"What's under the tarp?"

"Nosy, aren't you?" He snapped the reins and the horse shot forward, forcing Darla to clutch his thigh in order to keep from tumbling backward.

The unseasonably warm weather had deserted the area yesterday and temperatures had dipped into the upper forties. At least the sun took the bite out of the wind.

They bumped along in silence—Fletcher noted Darla hadn't released her grip on his leg. She'd been at the ranch three days and to his knowledge Danny hadn't confessed to her why he'd opened the ferret's cage. He admired the patience Darla showed with his son and admitted there was a part of him that hoped Danny wouldn't tell the truth so Darla would stick around a while longer.

He'd come to the realization today that he was going to stop fighting his feelings for Darla. Her willingness to help Danny proved that she cared about him and his son. How much he wasn't certain. For the time being caring was enough.

Once the ranch house disappeared from view, he asked, "Any luck with Danny today?"

"Yep."

He'd expected a *no* not a *yep*. "What did he say?"

"You won't like the answer."

Nothing with his son was ever easy. "Give it to me anyway."

"He wants me to help him convince Sandi to come home so the three of you can be a family again."

"What!" *Damn, you Sandi.* "I've told Danny a hundred different ways that his mother and I aren't reconciling. What more can I do?"

"This might be something that has to take its own course."

Fletcher cursed under his breath. "How does Danny expect you to help?"

"He wants me to take him shopping to buy a special gift for Sandi and then he intends to give her the present at the rodeo you're going to."

Fletcher took a deep breath, then exhaled slowly. "Sandi's been gone almost a year. How long can a kid keep hoping?"

"I don't know." Her blue eyes shone with compassion and Fletcher swore he'd been the biggest idiot in the world not fighting for Darla after he'd screwed up all those years ago.

"Is that where we're headed?"

All thoughts of Danny's troubles disappeared when Darla pointed to the old line shack that had been used as a storage shed for years. "Yep."

After Fletcher had married he'd spent months renovating the shelter. He'd needed breathing room. A place to hide when things got heated on the home front. He'd erected a corral next to the line shack, then installed a few creature comforts—a portable shower and a composting toilet. An underground propane tank supplied hot water and gas for the stove and small fridge. In place of electric lights he used kerosene lamps.

He stopped the buckboard by the front door. "Welcome to the Hanky Panky Ranch, ma'am."

A slow, seductive smile spread across Darla's face and his stomach lurched with excitement. "Fletcher McFadden, you intend to seduce me, don't you?"

"Yes, ma'am, I do."

She hopped to the ground. "Fortunately you have the luck o' the Irish on your side."

"I do?"

"Yes. It just so happens I'm in the mood to be seduced." She sashayed into the cabin, leaving Fletcher seated on the buckboard with his mouth hanging wide open.

Chapter Six

Slivers of light peeked through the muslin curtain covering the lone window in the line shack. Dawn beckoned, but Darla wished the new day would recede and allow the night to linger a while longer. At the moment, she was right where she wanted to be—snuggled in bed with Fletcher. His body curled around hers, warming her heart and soul.

She'd never felt as safe and cherished in another man's arms as she did when Fletcher held her close.

Yesterday there had been no need for words. The tension that had been brewing between them since the day she'd walked into the drugstore had exploded in a fierce coupling that had left her stunned and breathless.

Afterward they'd picnicked on the bed, trading memories of the early years of their courtship. The stories spurred another round of lovemaking—this time a slow foray of tender kisses and gentle caresses. Fletcher's lovemaking had touched her deeply—his whispered endearments a balm to her feminine ego.

She'd woken in the middle of the night, surrounded by his scent, his hard body and the certainty that he was the reason she'd never been able to commit to another man. All these years her heart had never let go of Fletcher.

She'd forgiven Fletcher for his old transgressions but had refused to acknowledge that truth, fearing she'd be forced to put Fletcher behind her for good when deep down she hadn't wanted to let go of him.

Okay, so she still loved Fletcher. Was a future with him possible? Although she cared for Danny deeply, was she ready for instant motherhood? What if Danny didn't want a stepmother? And what about her career? There was no need for an EPA lawyer in Junket, Texas. Then there was the fact that she loved Dallas. Returning to a small town where everyone knew your business would be a huge adjustment. Was there a way to be together without her having to make all the allowances?

You're jumping the gun. He hasn't even mentioned marriage.

Her worries died a sudden death when a warm callused hand slid over her belly and cupped her breast. A whiskered chin burrowed in the crook of her neck and firm lips nibbled her ear. "'Mornin'," he said.

Ah, she could get used to spooning with Fletcher in the mornings.

"Stay for Christmas, Darla. Spend the holiday at the Rocking J with the McFadden men."

Darla held her breath to keep from shouting an immediate *yes*. When Sandi failed to visit the Rocking J over the holidays would Danny blame it on Darla's presence? Or would he appreciate Darla being there for him when his mother wasn't?

Then there was Fletcher. The more time she spent with him in and out of bed, the greater risk to her heart.

If she lost him a second time she wasn't sure her heart would recover. "I'm in the middle of a court case." The case didn't go to trial until March, but she had a meeting scheduled for the end of the week.

"You can use my office to work out of." He rolled her onto her back and nuzzled her mouth. "Unless you'd planned to spend the holiday with your parents."

"They're visiting my aunt in Virginia." Darla had been invited along, but she'd begged off using work as an excuse. She hadn't wanted to explain why she'd broken her engagement with Blake. She coiled a strand of Fletcher's hair around her finger. "I suppose I could work from the ranch."

"Good." Fletcher's kiss stole her breath, reminding her again that her heart had never given up on him.

"We'll all go to the rodeo in Midland on Saturday."

The rodeo Sandi was expected to attend. Darla wouldn't miss that for the world.

"Got glue on the bottom of your shoes?" Daniel McFadden asked when he walked into the kitchen.

Fletcher frowned at the absurd question.

His father shook his head and chuckled. "You've been staring out the window for the past hour."

Guilty as charged. "They should have been home an hour ago." Darla had driven Danny into Midland to shop for a Christmas gift to give Sandi at the rodeo tomorrow. He'd checked in twice with the duo on his cell phone and Darla had assured him they were having a great time at the mall. The background noise during one of the calls made him suspect Darla had taken his son to the arcade.

"Danny's had a good week, hasn't he?" His father poured himself a cup of coffee and sat at the table.

His son's improved behavior should have made Fletcher happy, instead he worried the boy was setting himself up for disappointment. After learning he wanted Darla's help to win his mother back, Fletcher had been tempted to have a heart-to-heart talk with Danny—to try for the hundredth time to explain that Sandi was never coming home.

There were moments when Fletcher resented being seen as the bad guy. Not long ago Danny had accused him of being mean to Sandi and that's why she'd run away from the family. Fletcher wanted to defend himself against the charge, but hadn't, knowing that Danny had lashed out because he was hurting inside.

Fletcher wished he could spare his son the pain, but in the end Danny would learn the hard way that no matter what he did or said, his mother would never be what he needed her to be. And when that day came, Danny would realize that his father had been, and always would be, there for him.

"Danny boy sure is trying to impress Darla."

"I know." Fletcher had stood back and watched his son do everything he could to please Darla, even finishing the homework he'd been given to complete during his suspension from school. All because Darla had promised to help Danny try to win his mother back—a mother who'd rejected him.

"So what's going on between you and Darla?"

"I'm not sure, Dad."

His father sputtered into his coffee cup.

"What was that for?"

"I know one thing for sure—you're in love with her."

"Not now, Dad." Fletcher wasn't in the mood to talk about his love life.

"You never got over that girl. I suspect Sandi knew, too."

All those wasted years. Fletcher felt a sense of urgency to make up for lost time with Darla. To make new memories. He knew she had feelings for him—otherwise she wouldn't have made love with him. But they weren't the same people they'd been in high school and he worried that Darla wouldn't give him a chance to prove he'd never let her down again.

"Do you expect Sandi to show up at the rodeo?"

"She'd better." J.T. Riker was slated to compete in the bull riding event and Sandi was never far from the man's side. Since she'd claimed she couldn't get away to see her son over the Christmas break, Fletcher had bullied her into agreeing to spend the afternoon with Danny at the rodeo. Danny was under the impression his mother wanted him there.

Danny loved the rodeo and that irked Fletcher. He and Logan had entered a few rodeos in high school but neither had been any good at the sport. They'd stuck with football and basketball instead. Speaking of Logan, Fletcher owed his friend a call. He'd been so wrapped up in Darla's visit and handling Danny's expulsion from school that he'd forgotten to return his friend's calls.

You're making excuses.

Fearing he'd jinx his relationship with Darla, Fletcher hadn't wanted to tell Logan that his high school flame had returned to town. Logan would ask if Fletcher intended to take Darla to Junket's annual Christmas parade tomorrow. He wasn't ready to show up with Darla and have to answer everyone's nosy questions about their relationship—mostly because he didn't have the answers to those questions.

"J.T.'S THE BEST bull rider in the whole world, right Dad?" Danny glanced at his father.

Fletcher mumbled something incoherent and buried his face in the rodeo program. Darla could understand why he didn't want to talk about the bull rider. "Is that what you want to be when you grow up—a bull rider?" she asked Danny.

Nodding, the boy shoved a handful of popcorn into his mouth. She caught Fletcher's eye and smiled. "Must be from growing up around all those bulls you raise on the ranch."

Another snort. Good grief, what was the matter with Fletcher? Her gaze dropped to the gift bag peeking out from beneath Danny's seat and she suspected his agitation resulted from worrying over how Sandi would treat Danny today.

This morning after breakfast she and Danny had carefully wrapped the gift they'd bought for his mother. Danny's excitement was heartbreaking and Darla prayed Sandi wouldn't disappoint the boy.

When the announcer introduced the bullfighters—the cowboys who willingly threw themselves in harm's way to protect the competitors—Darla focused on the events in the arena and forced her worries to the back of her mind.

"Be sure to stop by the Resistol Relief Fund booth outside the arena. Your donations provide financial aid to rodeo cowboys whose careers have been put on hold due to injuries sustained during competition," the announcer said.

Danny tugged her shirt sleeve. "Miss Darla?" He licked his cherry-stained lips and bit off another piece of the licorice rope Fletcher had bought from a candy vendor.

She'd told Danny to call her Miss Darla because Ms. Baker made her feel old. "What, honey?" The endearment slipped out, but if Danny noticed he gave no indication.

"Dad says when I get older I can go to cowboy school and learn how to ride a bull."

"How old do you have to be to go to one of those schools?"

"Twelve."

Twelve? That seemed too young.

"Ladies and gentlemen, we're about to begin the bull-riding competition at the twenty-third annual Hoe-Down Rodeo. We Texans claim bull riding as America's first extreme sport!"

The arena erupted in applause and cheers.

"Folks, there's plenty of excitement ahead. The cowboys are gearing up in the bucking chutes." Spotlights highlighted the riders taping their gloves to their wrists and rubbing the leather with rosin, a sticky substance for extra gripping power.

"For those of you watching your first bull-riding event there's four judges who have fifty points each to award—twenty-five go to the bull and twenty-five go to the rider. The total from each of the judges is added together, then divided by two to get the rider and bull score. A perfect ride is a hundred points."

The bullfighters in the arena did a series of gymnastics moves and entertained the crowd for a few minutes before the announcer continued. "Twelve cowboys have entered today's event and we're savin' the best for last— J.T. Riker! Riker's recent ride in Wyoming a week ago earned him a first place in the standings. He's tanglin' with Blood Bath today. That bull's been known to draw blood from more 'n a few cowboys."

Cheers followed.

"Folks, shift your attention to chute three. Eric Storm's ridin' Red Rage. Eric needs a score of 83 or better to reach the finals. Red Rage swings to left. Let's see if this cowboy hangs on for the full eight seconds."

The gate opened and Red Rage exploded from the chute. As the announcer predicted, the auburn-colored bull swung left and kicked his back legs furiously, trying to shed the flank strap. When the bull spun in the opposite direction, the cowboy lost his balance. As he slid sideways, his free hand came in contact with the bull. The buzzer sounded and the bullfighters coaxed Red Rage out of the arena, while the cowboy stumbled to safety.

"Bad luck for Eric Storm. His free hand touched the bull, which disqualifies his ride. Better luck next time, cowboy."

Ten more riders came and went—thank goodness none of them got hurt—Darla didn't have the stomach for blood nor did she care to see a man hung up on a bull's horn and flung around like a rag doll.

"As promised, the final bull ride of the day belongs to J. T. Riker—Midland's hometown hero!" The JumboTron flashed a close-up of the bull rider in chute five. Riker was pure rodeo cowboy. Handsome and rugged— a jagged scar ran along his jaw, adding an aura of danger to his looks. Shaggy, black hair peeked from beneath the cowboy hat.

Speaking of looks…Fletcher scowled at her. Was he jealous? The idea held some appeal. Never hurt for a man to worry where his woman's thoughts strayed.

"Let's hope J.T. hangs on today and avoids the horns."

"Miss Darla." Danny tapped his finger against her thigh, then pointed to the chute where the cowboy wrapped and unwrapped the bull rope around his left hand. "J.T. doesn't wear a vest or a helmet, but Dad says I gotta wear one if I'm gonna be a bull rider when I grow up."

Before she offered her opinion on the use of protective gear, the chute opened. The bull whipped the cowboy from side to side and Darla feared the man's spine would snap in two before the ride ended. Eight seconds lasted forever, then the buzzer rang and the bullfighters rushed the bull, while the cowboy loosened his hand from the rope and jumped to safety. J.T. hit the ground and rolled, then launched himself at the arena rails and climbed out of the way of the bull's horns in the nick of time.

"Eighty-eight, folks. J. T. Riker's headin' home tonight with a little jingle in his pocket."

While the crowd applauded and Danny waved his miniature U.S. flag in the air, Fletcher texted on his cell phone. After a moment he glanced her way. "Everything okay?" she asked.

"Yeah." He checked his watch. "In five minutes Danny and I need to be out on the concourse."

He must have sent Sandi a text message to meet them. Darla considered waiting in her seat for Fletcher to return, but decided she'd go to support Danny, because she knew the boy worried that his mother wouldn't like the Christmas present he had for her. Fletcher reached beneath his seat for the gift bag. He handed it to Danny, then led the way to an exit. The solemn expression on Fletcher's face worried Darla as the three waited outside the bathrooms on the main concourse.

"There's Mom!" Danny pointed to a group of spectators heading their way.

Sandi Rutledge strolled toward them, wearing painted-on jeans, a western blouse with fringe that swung across her generous bosom with each step. Her jeans were tucked into red boots. With her long blond hair and heavy makeup she blended right in with the rodeo groupies.

"Oh, my, gosh." Sandi stopped in front of them. "Darla Baker?" She motioned to Darla's hair. "Wow, you cut it all off." She glanced between Darla and Fletcher, her dark blond eyebrows arching.

Darla was appalled—not at Sandi's shallowness, but the fact that she hadn't greeted her son, who hopped up and down in an attempt to gain his mother's attention.

"Look, Mom," Danny said, holding up the Christmas bag.

"What's that?" Sandi hadn't even hugged her son.

"I got you a Christmas present." He thrust the bag at her.

"Oh, well isn't that nice."

"Aren't you gonna open it?"

"Sure." Sandi dug through the tissue paper and removed the framed twelve-by-sixteen picture.

"That's me, Mom. Miss Darla took me to the mall and there was this man who could draw cartoons and he—"

"Oh, how silly." Sandi dropped the picture into the gift bag.

Danny's chin quivered and Darla had to force herself not to hug the boy. "Don't you like it?" he asked.

"Of course." Sandi glanced at Fletcher, whose hands were balled into fists. "I'm on the road with J.T. all the time now and there's not much room in his camper." Sandi held the bag out to her ex. "Will you keep this until…" She smiled at Danny. "Well, until we have a chance to visit again?"

"Didn't you get me a Christmas present?" Danny asked his mother.

Sandi glanced nervously at Fletcher. "Ah…" She looked around. "Be right back." Leaving the gift bag on the concourse floor she flounced over to a hat booth and selected a boy's tan cowboy hat. She returned to the group and offered it to Danny. "How's this for a Christmas present?"

Danny didn't smile. "I already got a hat."

"Oh, but this one's special."

"It is?"

"This one will have J.T.'s autograph on it."

"Really?" Danny grinned.

If Fletcher's jaw tightened any more the bone would splinter and poke through his cheek.

"Here comes J.T. now." Sandi shouted his name. "Over here, love!"

Oh, gross. Darla barely managed to refrain from rolling her eyes.

The bull rider made his way toward the group,

stopping every few feet to sign his name to a T-shirt, a hat or a woman's bare tummy. "Miss me, darlin'?" He pulled Sandi against him and kissed her.

Fletcher's reaction appeared more annoyed than jealous. Any worries that he had feelings for his ex-wife were put to rest with this encounter. "Danny wants to visit with you for a while," Fletcher said. The two men hadn't shook hands. As a matter of fact J.T. avoided making eye contact with Fletcher. At least the bull rider had the decency to look a little embarrassed.

"We'll be around." Fletcher grabbed Darla's hand. They'd taken two steps when Sandi called after them. "Wait!" She flashed a smile at Danny. "Um, I can't visit with Danny today. J.T. and I are leaving."

"Gotta catch another rodeo." J.T. grinned. "You know how it is for us top contenders."

"Dad said you and J.T. would take me to see the bulls," Danny whined.

Sandi straightened the boy's shirt collar. "Maybe next time."

"When?" Danny crossed his arms over his skinny chest.

"I don't know when, Danny."

"But you're coming home for Christmas, right?"

"Not this year. J.T.'s got a big rodeo in California next week. But I'll call you."

Danny's gaze dropped to the floor and Darla felt a surge of anger rush through her at the horrible way Sandi rejected her son. No wonder Fletcher couldn't stand the woman. Darla settled her hand on Danny's shoulder not caring that Sandi noticed and smirked.

"Oh, before I forget. J.T., will you autograph Danny's hat? It's his Christmas present."

"Sure thing."

J.T. reached for the hat, but Danny flung it at the ground. "I don't wanna dumb hat." The boy stormed away.

"Nice going, Sandi," Fletcher muttered, then took off after Danny.

Shocked by the exchange, Darla stared.

"What?" Sandi snapped.

Darla had no intentions of getting involved in an argument with Sandi. "If you don't want the picture, then I'll take it for Fletcher." She motioned to the bag with the character sketch of Danny inside.

"Whatever." Sandi grabbed the bull rider's arm and they walked off, swallowed up by another crowd of rodeo groupies.

Darla found the McFadden males standing in a concession line, Danny clutching Fletcher's thigh. "Time for lunch?"

Fletcher grunted and avoided eye contact with her. They ordered hot dogs, onion rings and drinks, then sat at one of the tables along the concourse. Danny ate in silence, swinging his legs beneath the table and staring into space. Fletcher kept his gaze on his food. Darla searched for a way to salvage the day.

"Hey, Danny," she said.

"What?"

"How would you like to skip the rest of the rodeo and go see the old trucks at the Fire Museum downtown?"

The boy shrugged.

"You can sit in the trucks and try on the firemen's gear. Even slide down the fire pole."

"Okay." Although his response was unenthusiastic,

Danny made short work of his meal. "Done," he announced a few minutes later.

Amused and thankful the child's spirit hadn't been too badly damaged by his mother's rebuff, Darla said, "As soon as I finish my onion rings."

Danny snatched the last onion ring and stuffed it into his mouth. "Okay. You're done now." He flashed a sweet ketchup-stained grin.

Lord, how easy it would be to love this child as if he were her own. No matter that Danny resembled Sandi. He was a part of Fletcher—a man her heart refused to forget.

"Thanks," Fletcher said. A whole lot more than gratitude shone in his eyes when he squeezed her hand.

Chapter Seven

"Mom's never coming back, is she?" Danny asked when Fletcher closed the *Harry Potter* book Saturday night. The rodeo, the trip to the fire museum and a pit stop at an arcade on the way home from Midland had worn the boy out and he hadn't protested when Fletcher announced his bedtime.

"No, Danny, your mom's not going to ever live with us." A father should be able to protect his son from the emotional pain and hurt of neglect, but he was tired of making excuses for his ex-wife.

"Mom likes J.T. better 'n me, doesn't she?" The wobble in his little voice cut Fletcher to the core.

"Your mom loves you, she just doesn't show it very well." Fletcher hugged his son close.

"I wish Miss Darla was my mom."

The announcement surprised Fletcher. "You weren't very nice to Miss Darla when you first met her."

Danny picked at a piece of lint on the bed covering. "I didn't want you to like her because I wanted you to like Mom again."

"Danny, your mom and I don't love each other anymore and that's not going to change."

"Can't you try to love each other again?"

Fletcher's heart ached for his son. "It doesn't work like that."

"Grandpa said you used to love Miss Darla a long time ago."

What kind of talks were his father and son having these days? "Miss Darla and I were very close when we were growing up."

"Are you gonna try to love Miss Darla?"

Try? Fletcher had never stopped loving Darla. "Love is complicated, Danny." He really didn't want to have this conversation with a seven-year-old.

"Is Darla gonna be my new mom?" Danny's eyes shined with hope.

Fletcher wished he could promise his son a new mom but he hadn't brought up the subject of marriage with Darla because he hadn't figured out a way to work out the logistics.

"Miss Darla lives in Dallas, buddy, and that's a long way from Junket. She's got a very important job and we can't ask her to quit that."

"Can we go live with her in Dallas?"

Fletcher had tossed that scenario around in his mind the past few days and he didn't see how he could make it work. His father couldn't handle the ranch on his own. *There's enough money to hire a foreman to run the operation when you're not here.*

He'd have to commute every two weeks or so and spend a few days at the Rocking J keeping the books and handling any problems that cropped up. *Buy a small commuter jet and fly back and forth as often as you need to.*

But what about his father? He hated leaving him alone especially after he'd gotten used to having Danny underfoot all the time.

He and Darla get along great. Buy a bigger place in Dallas and Dad can visit as often and for as long as he wants.

"How would you feel about starting over in a different school and having to make new friends?"

The sparkle in Danny's eyes fizzled out. "Do I have to go to a new school because I broke the rule in the science lab and let Fred out of his cage?"

"No. If Miss Darla and I got married, we'd have to move to Dallas." Danny didn't understand how far apart Dallas and Junket were.

"What about Grandpa? Would he go to Dallas with us?"

"If he wants to."

"I guess I can make new friends." Danny sat up straight in bed. "And it's okay if Darla wants to be my new mom. I told her I was gonna be a fireman when I grew up and she said that was a really important job."

"I thought you wanted to be a bull rider?"

Danny shrugged. Looked as if the famous J. T. Riker had fallen off his pedestal. "Dad?"

"What?"

"Can you ask Miss Darla to marry us?"

You read my mind, son. He yearned to recapture the years he and Darla had lost. But he hated to get his son's hope up that Darla might become a permanent part of their lives. "I'm glad you like Miss Darla, Danny. We'll see how things go, okay?"

"Are you gonna buy Miss Darla a Christmas present?"

"Yep." He'd had one in mind all week and planned to drive into Midland on Monday and shop. He tucked the blankets around his son. "Better get some shut-eye."

"'Night, Dad."

Outside Danny's room, Fletcher leaned against the wall and rubbed his brow. He knew what he wanted—a do-over with Darla. But if he flubbed it up with her again, he wouldn't be the only one hurting. He had to consider what was best for Danny. His son had already been abandoned by one mother and he'd become attached to Darla in a short time. In Fletcher's mind there was really only one solution—marriage. Now he just had to convince Darla they could make it work.

"Everything okay?" Darla's whispered question came from the top of the stairs.

How long had she stood watching him? He pushed away from the wall, grabbed her hand and promptly pulled her into his arms and kissed the daylights out of her.

He took his time, wanting to convey with his kiss how much she meant to him. How much he appreciated her suggestion they visit the fire museum. He wanted her to know he loved her for treating his son the way a real mother should. He wanted her to know he was proud of her career accomplishments. How attractive he found her. How he couldn't stop thinking about making love to her again. How much he wanted her to be a part of the rest of his life. Eventually they had to come up for air.

"Wow." Her breath puffed against his lips. "What did I do to deserve that?"

Tell her. He wanted to. But when he spilled his guts,

he intended to follow with a ring and a proposal. "That was for saving the day." He smoothed the wrinkle that formed between her eyebrows. "Danny had a great time at the museum. Now he wants to be a firefighter when he grows up."

"I'm sorry Sandi hurt his feelings." Darla snuggled her head beneath his chin. "And I'm sorry she hurt you."

"I guess you figured out J.T. Riker was the man Sandi had the affair with."

Darla nodded against his chest. He grabbed her hand and led her downstairs. "What do you say we bundle up in our coats and sit by the pool?"

"Sure."

Once outside, Fletcher switched on the stone fire pit, then dragged a lounge chair closer to the flames. He stretched out and snuggled Darla in his lap. For a while they enjoyed the peace and quiet and stared at the stars.

"Tell me about the guys you were engaged to."

"Richard was in law school with me. Benjamin, I met through a friend. He was an accountant. And Blake is a lawyer at the firm."

All professionals—none of them bull breeders.

"Mind if I ask why those relationships didn't work out?" At her hesitation he said, "I expected you to be married and have a few kids by now."

"The truth?" she whispered.

"Always." He was done with lies. He'd experienced enough dishonesty in his marriage.

"None of those men were you."

Her declaration soothed his ego, but at the same time scared the hell out of him. She hadn't said the words, but her confession came close. He clasped Darla's face between his hands and kissed her, allowing her sweet taste to calm his anxiety.

"I need to tell you something," she said.

"What?"

"I have to go back to Dallas."

"You said you'd stay until Christmas." Danny wouldn't be the only one who'd be crushed if Darla wasn't here to open presents with them on Christmas morning.

"Something's come up at work."

"I thought things had slowed down at the office?"

"They have but I scheduled a meeting with my boss next Wednesday. It was the only day he could fit me in before he leaves on vacation for two weeks."

Fletcher's insides twisted into a knot. Was he going too fast for her? Had he said or done something to provoke second thoughts about their relationship?

"I could go with you?" He feared if he let her out of his sight he'd lose her.

"That's sweet, but I won't have time to spend with you. Besides, you need to be here with Danny."

He shrugged. "Danny can come along. We'll find stuff to do while you're working."

Darla wiggled out of his arms and stood. "I need to go alone, Fletcher. I plan to leave early in the morning before Danny wakes."

He watched her head into the house, and the question on the tip of his tongue—Is this goodbye?— never left his mouth.

"I CAN'T BELIEVE you're leaving?"

Darla spun and found her coworker, Anna Crane, standing in the office doorway. "Me neither."

"The guy must be pretty special if you're handing over the wetlands case to Harry. Especially after you laid all the groundwork."

"The guy—" Darla smiled "—is indeed a very special cowboy."

"I wish I could find a cowboy willing to put up with my long hours." Anna blew her bangs off her forehead. "You're going to kill me for asking this but are you sure this time?"

Darla deserved the question. She'd cried on Anna's shoulder through three engagements and three breakups. "Yep, Fletcher's the one. He's been the one since the very beginning."

"When's the wedding?" Anna asked.

"I don't know."

"Whoa, wait a minute." Anna moved across the room and sat in the chair at Darla's desk. "You put your condo on the market and he hasn't asked you to marry him?"

She'd worked tirelessly to realize her dream of becoming a lawyer, but in the end she'd paid a high price. She possessed a fulfilling career but her personal life was nothing to brag about. No husband. No children. Her day-to-day existence consisted of endless work hours with a few vacations thrown into the mix. "Who says he has to be the one to ask?"

Darla believed if she were to have a chance at her own happy-ever-after, then she'd need to make a few sacrifices—the biggest being she'd move back to Junket.

"You're going to propose?"

"Yes." There was no way she'd ask Fletcher to move Danny to a new school in Dallas when the boy was having trouble adjusting to his mother's absence. And the idea of leaving Fletcher's father alone on the ranch didn't sit well with Darla.

She wanted to make the sacrifices needed for her and Fletcher to have a future. Practicing law was important to her and she didn't want to walk away from her career, but she was willing to prove how much she loved Fletcher by cutting back on courtroom appearances and reverting to a behind-the-scenes role, helping the other lawyers in the firm prepare their cases. That would leave her plenty of time to be a wife and a mother.

"When do you plan to—" Anna rolled her eyes "—ask for his hand in marriage?"

"I'm leaving in the morning. I intend to spend Christmas Eve with the McFadden men."

"Did someone mention the McFadden men?"

Darla gasped and Anna popped out of the chair. Both women stared at Fletcher in surprise.

"We didn't mean to scare you, Miss Darla," Danny said, peeking around his father.

"Ah…Anna, I'd like you to meet Fletcher McFadden and his son Danny."

Anna smiled. "Nice to meet you both." She glanced at Darla. "Keep in touch." Then headed for the door. "Merry Christmas, gentlemen," she said, skirting past them.

As soon as Anna left the office Danny raced across the room and jumped in the chair. "Guess what, Miss Darla?"

"What, honey?"

"Dad and I are gonna move to Dallas."

Darla's face paled and anxiety gnawed away at Fletcher's confidence. Had he jumped the gun?

"I don't understand," she said.

Fletcher prayed for the right words. He moved closer,

stopping next to her. "What Danny's trying to say is you mean the world to us and we don't want to lose you."

"Wait!" She pressed her palm to his chest, her gaze glancing back and forth between him and Danny. "You can't do this."

"Do what?" he asked.

"Do…do what I think you're about to do."

He grinned. "What is it you *think* I'm about to do?"

"You're going to do what I'd planned to do."

Danny's face scrunched into a frown. "What's she talking about, Dad?"

"Maybe we should let Miss Darla tell us." He shifted closer, invading her personal space, inhaling her sexy perfume and sweet scent.

"I was packing my things," she said.

For the first time since entering her office, Fletcher paid attention to his surroundings. He noticed the cardboard box on her desk filled with coffee mugs, a plant, picture frames and other junk. The hairs on the back of his neck stood on end. Was she running from him?

"Where are you planning to go?" he asked.

"Home."

Danny beat him to the question. "What home?"

Darla's eyes glowed as she set aside the paperweight she held and stared Fletcher in the eye. "Home as in the Rocking J."

Relief swept through him, leaving his limbs shaky. He swallowed twice but the words stuck to the sides of his swollen throat.

"I knew when I saw your photo on MySpace," she continued. "That you were the reason I couldn't commit to other men. I'd never gotten over you. Being with you these past weeks confirmed that…" She shook her head.

"What?" The word escaped his mouth in a husky whisper.

"That you haven't changed. You're the same sensitive, wonderful, caring, generous guy I fell in love with back in high school. The same guy I never stopped loving."

"And…"

"And I don't want to live without you. I want that happy-ever-after that was meant for the two of us from the beginning." She placed her hand over his heart. "I'm saying…marry me, cowboy."

"What about me, Miss Darla? Are you gonna marry me, too?"

Darla held her hand out and Danny jumped off the chair and joined the adults. "Yes, Danny. I'll marry you, too, if you'll have me."

"Have you what, Miss Darla?"

"Have me as your mother."

"Cool. That's what Dad said you'd be if you married us."

Fletcher couldn't stand it any longer. He pulled Darla close and brushed his lips across hers, saving the *big kiss* for later in private.

"Yuck." Danny lost interest in the adults and rummaged through the box, giving Fletcher a moment to speak his heart.

"I love you, Darla Baker, and yes, I'll marry you."

"This time everything will work out and we'll be happy, won't we, Fletch?" Her breath sighed against his neck as he hugged her close.

"I won't take you for granted, Darla. Every day I'll show you in as many ways as possible how much I love you and how grateful I am for this second chance with you. But—"

"There's a but?"

"But I don't expect you to give up your career at the law firm. I talked it over with Danny and he's willing to move here and go to a new school. I'll commute back to the ranch when needed to help Dad with the bulls. And we're hiring a ranch manager to run things while I'm in Dallas. Dad and I worked it all out."

"Your father doesn't mind you and Danny moving so far away?"

"He's always believed you and I were meant to be together and he wants us to be happy."

"What are you going to do all day when I'm at work and Danny's in school?" she asked.

"I don't know." He grinned. "I can always fool around on MySpace."

"Oh, no. *My* used-car salesman is not going to flirt with big-haired blondes."

"What's a flirt?" Danny asked.

The little stinker had big ears. "Someone who says nice things to another person," Darla explained.

"I told Mrs. Tuttle that her red shoes were cool. Does that mean I'm a flirt?"

Fletcher chuckled. "No, that was just being nice." He rubbed his finger across Darla's lower lip. "Danny and I drove up here to bring you back to the ranch for Christmas. We missed you and didn't want to spend the holiday without you."

"I'd planned to leave in the morning for Junket."

"Sounds good. In the meantime, can Danny and I bunk at your condo tonight?"

"You can bunk with me anywhere, cowboy."

CHURCH SERVICE Christmas Eve was packed. Ushers directed the McFaddens to a pew in the middle of the sanctuary. Fletcher was a wreck. Tonight it was his turn to propose to Darla. He had it all planned out... A roaring fire. A bottle of champagne. And the engagement ring he'd bought in Midland for her the day she'd returned to Dallas. He'd known then that he wasn't going to let anything keep them apart. And to be sure he'd covered all the bases he'd purchased a box of fancy chocolates and a fresh bouquet of flowers.

For the umpteenth time his gaze shifted to the woman who'd possessed his heart since kindergarten. Darla took his breath away in the knee-length black cocktail dress with a glittering rhinestone jacket. Fletcher had noticed the envious stares of other men when they'd entered the church.

Mrs. Polanski tapped his shoulder and slipped him a folded note.

We need to talk. Meet me by the pond tomorrow at noon. L.T.

Fletcher swiveled in his seat and spotted Logan Taylor sitting three pews back with Cassidy Ortiz and her mother. *Cassidy Ortiz?* When had his friend and the local hairdresser become an item?

The fact that Logan was present tonight was a miracle in and of itself. Until now, the man hadn't stepped foot inside the church since his wife had died. He nodded, signaling he'd gotten the message. Logan stared point-edly at Darla, then quirked an eyebrow.

Yeah, they'd both kept secrets from each other.

Right then the children's choir broke into song and Fletcher grasped Darla's hand, noticing his son held her other hand. The McFadden men were definitely staking their claim on Darla.

An hour later the service ended and Fletcher whisked his family out of church, bypassing the long line of well-wishers. Once they arrived at the ranch Darla made hot chocolate for everyone and Danny fixed a plate of cookies for Santa. They sat on the couch in the family room in front of the fireplace, a Christmas CD playing softly in the background. Fletcher's father had retired early to his room to watch TV before going to bed.

"Dad, can I give Miss Darla her Christmas present now?"

"Don't you want to wait until tomorrow?" Fletcher asked.

"Nope."

"It's up to Darla."

Darla hugged Danny close. "You bought me a Christmas present?"

"You've already seen it but—"

"Why don't you let Darla open it first before you spill the beans and tell her what it is," Fletcher said.

Danny slipped behind the tree, then reappeared with a wrapped gift. Fletcher suspected Darla knew what it was but she made a big production of tearing off the paper a little bit at a time until Danny was hopping up and down with excitement.

Darla gasped. "I get to have this for myself?" She

examined the cartoon sketch of Danny that Sandi hadn't cared to keep.

"It's supposed to be for my mom, remember?" Danny asked shyly.

"I do remember."

"Now you're gonna be my mom, too, so I want you to have it."

"This is the best Christmas present I've ever received. Thank you." She hugged Danny.

Danny stared expectantly at her and Darla cast a questioning glance at Fletcher. "What is it, Danny?" he asked.

"Isn't she gonna hang it up somewhere?"

"Not tonight. Time for bed." Fletcher stood. "Santa won't stop at this house unless you're asleep."

"Okay." He gave Darla one more hug. "You're gonna be here in the morning, right?"

"You bet." Darla kissed the top of his head. "Sweet dreams, honey."

"Brush your teeth," Fletcher called out as Danny climbed the stairs.

"Finally we're alone." Fletcher grinned. "Be right back." He headed into the kitchen and grabbed the champagne. "Did I tell you how beautiful you look tonight?" he said, returning to the living room.

She smiled. "Only a thousand times."

He set the bubbly and glasses on the coffee table. "Hang on. There's more." A second later he reappeared with the box of chocolates and bouquet of flowers.

"Flowers?" She buried her nose in the petals. "What are you up to, Fletch?"

"You had your say yesterday. Now it's my turn." He rummaged under the tree and picked up a small silver-wrapped gift. "First, I'm going to kiss you because I've been dying to all night long."

The kiss began slowly with little nibbles, but desire took over and soon he kissed Darla like a man on a mission—to coax her into his bed. They were both breathing hard when he pulled away. He handed her the gift. "Open it."

She tore the paper off and lifted the lid of the black velvet box. Her breath caught and tears welled in her eyes. "It's beautiful."

He removed the ring and grasped Darla's left hand in his. "We've waited a long time to be together. Let's not look back anymore. From now on, the only road we're traveling is the road in front of us." He slid the ring onto her finger. "I love you, Darla. Will you marry me?"

"I love you, too, Fletcher." She brushed her mouth across his and whispered, "Yes, I'll marry you."

As far as Christmas Eves went, Santa couldn't top this one.

Epilogue

"Was wonderin' if you'd show up," Logan said, sitting atop the split-rail fence fifty yards from the watering hole.

Fletcher tied his horse next to Logan's and hopped up on the fence.

"If that grin of yours gets any wider, your face'll rip apart."

"Appears I'm not the only one who's got something to smile about."

Logan fought to keep a straight face but after a few seconds he gave in and chuckled. Fletcher joined him and the two cowboys hooted and hollered until they were forced to wipe their eyes on their shirtsleeves.

"So what's this I hear about you becoming a father?" Fletcher asked.

"If you'd have returned my damned calls you'd know."

"Yeah, well, as you noticed in church last night I had other things on my mind besides shooting the bull with you."

Logan shook his head. "So your online Daisy turned out to be Darla Baker."

"Nope. Pure coincidence that Darla walked into the drugstore the day I was supposed to meet Daisy."

"What happened with Daisy?"

"Nothing. She decided I wasn't her type."

Logan quirked an eyebrow.

"I was relieved because once I saw Darla, Daisy was history."

"So Darla's not married?"

"Nope. She came close a time or two but it turns out she couldn't stop thinking about me." Fletcher grinned, then became serious. "I'm getting a second chance with her, Logan, but I'm scared as hell I'll blow it."

"Me, too." Logan stared into space. "I never thought I'd love another woman after Bethany. I wasn't looking for one when Cassidy walked into Billie's Roadhouse last September and hauled my drunken ass home and put me to bed."

"I'm guessing she hopped in that bed with you," Fletcher said.

"Woke up and couldn't remember a damned thing. Three months later Cassidy tells me I'm going to be a father. 'Bout scared the bejeezes out of me." Logan glanced at Fletcher. "I'm worried something will happen to her and the baby."

"If there's one thing I've learned, hoss, it's that life doesn't come with guarantees. We live it one day at a time and never take for granted those we love."

"You and Darla plan to tie the knot?"

"Yep. We're going to live at the Rocking J and Darla's going to cut back on her hours and do some consulting work for the law firm." He elbowed Logan. "We hope to start a family soon. Give yours and Cassidy's rug rat a playmate."

"How's Danny taking the news he's getting a new mother?"

"He's smitten with Darla." Silence stretched between the men, then Fletcher asked, "What are you and Cassidy planning to do?"

"We're getting married, too. I'm not sure what's going to happen with her mother."

"What's wrong with Cassidy's mother?"

"She's got Alzheimer's."

"Man, that's rough."

Logan nodded. "I've been thinking about hauling Cassidy's trailer and hair salon out to my place and setting it up next to the house. That way her mother would be close by and Cassidy could keep cutting hair."

"Sounds like a good idea."

"Cassidy's pretty tight with her elderly neighbors. I might have to haul their trailer out to the ranch, too."

Fletcher slapped Logan on the back. "Pretty soon we'll be calling your place the Rockin' Chair Ranch."

"Real funny." Logan grunted, but deep down he didn't give one whit if there were a hundred trailers filled with old farts parked on his property. As long as he and Cassidy were together nothing else mattered.

"Hey, maybe we should have a double wedding," Fletcher said.

"I'm steering clear of wedding plans. That's Cassidy's deal."

"I'll talk to Darla and see what she thinks. We can have our weddings at the church and a big shindig out at the Rocking J. That ought to keep the Junket tongues wagging."

"I don't know if I'm ready for all that hoopla. I was hoping for a justice-of-the-peace ceremony."

"Our gals have waited a long time for their turn to walk down the aisle."

Logan sighed. "I guess I'll survive a church wedding if it makes Cassidy happy."

Both men stared into space, their thoughts on the women who had lassoed their hearts. Fletcher scraped the bottom of his boot against the rail. "Turned out to be a pretty good Christmas for a couple of down-n-out cowboys like us."

"Merry Christmas, Fletcher."

"Merry Christmas, hoss."

*Bestselling author Lynne Graham is back
with a fabulous new trilogy!*

PREGNANT BRIDES

Three ordinary girls—naive, but also honest and plucky…

*Three fabulously wealthy, impossibly handsome
and very ruthless men…*

*When opposites attract and passion leads to pregnancy…
it can only mean marriage!*

*Available next month from Harlequin Presents®:
the first installment*

DESERT PRINCE, BRIDE OF INNOCENCE

* * *

'THIS EVENING I'm flying to New York for two weeks,'
Jasim imparted with a casualness that made her heart sink
like a stone. 'That's why I had you brought here. I own this
apartment and you'll be comfortable here while I'm abroad.'

'I can afford my own accommodation although I may not
need it for long. I'll have another job by the time you
get back—'

Jasim released a slightly harsh laugh. 'There's no need for
you to look for another position. How would I ever see you?
Don't you understand what I'm offering you?'

Elinor stood very still. 'No, I must be incredibly thick
because I haven't quite worked out yet what you're offering
me.…'

His charismatic smile slashed his lean dark visage.
'Naturally, I want to take care of you.…'

'No, thanks.' Elinor forced a smile and mentally willed him not to demean her with some sordid proposition. 'The only man who will ever take *care* of me with my agreement will be my husband. I'm willing to wait for you to come back but I'm not willing to be kept by you. I'm a very independent woman and what I give, I give freely.'

Jasim frowned. 'You make it all sound so serious.'

'What happened between us last night left pure chaos in its wake. Right now, I don't know whether I'm on my head or my heels. I'll stay for a while because I have nowhere else to go in the short term. So maybe it's good that you'll be away for a while.'

Jasim pulled out his wallet to extract a card. 'My private number,' he told her, presenting her with it as though it was a precious gift, which indeed it was. Many women would have done just about anything to gain access to that direct hotline to him, but his staff guarded his privacy with scrupulous care.

Before he could close the wallet, his blood ran cold in his veins. How could he have made such a serious oversight? What if he had got her pregnant? He knew that an unplanned pregnancy would engulf his life like an avalanche, crush his freedom and suffocate him. He barely stilled a shudder at the threat of such an outcome and thought how ironic it was that what his older brother had longed and prayed for to secure the line to the throne should strike Jasim as an absolute disaster....

* * *

What will proud Prince Jasim do if Elinor is expecting his royal baby? Perhaps an arranged marriage is the only solution! But will Elinor agree? Find out in DESERT PRINCE, BRIDE OF INNOCENCE by Lynne Graham [#2884], available from Harlequin Presents® in January 2010.

HARLEQUIN *Presents*

Bestselling Harlequin Presents author

Lynne Graham

brings you an exciting new miniseries:

PREGNANT BRIDES

Inexperienced and expecting, they're forced to marry

Collect them all:

DESERT PRINCE, BRIDE OF INNOCENCE
January 2010

RUTHLESS MAGNATE, CONVENIENT WIFE
February 2010

GREEK TYCOON, INEXPERIENCED MISTRESS
March 2010

New Year, New Man!

*For the perfect New Year's punch,
blend the following:*

- *One woman determined to find her inner vixen*
- *A notorious—and notoriously hot!—playboy*
- *A provocative New Year's Eve bash*
- *An impulsive kiss that leads to a night of
explosive passion!*

When the clock hits midnight Claire Daniels
kisses the guy standing closest to her, but
the kiss doesn't end after the bells stop ringing....

Look for

Moonstruck

by *USA TODAY* bestselling author

JULIE KENNER

Available January

red-hot reads

REQUEST YOUR FREE BOOKS!

2 FREE NOVELS PLUS 2 FREE GIFTS!

HARLEQUIN®

American ★ Romance®

Love, Home & Happiness!

YES! Please send me 2 FREE Harlequin® American Romance® novels and my 2 FREE gifts (gifts are worth about $10). After receiving them, if I don't wish to receive any more books, I can return the shipping statement marked "cancel." If I don't cancel, I will receive 4 brand-new novels every month and be billed just $4.24 per book in the U.S. or $4.99 per book in Canada.* That's a savings of close to 15% off the cover price! It's quite a bargain! Shipping and handling is just 50¢ per book. I understand that accepting the 2 free books and gifts places me under no obligation to buy anything. I can always return a shipment and cancel at any time. Even if I never buy another book from Harlequin, the two free books and gifts are mine to keep forever.

154 HDN E4DS 354 HDN E4D4

Name	(PLEASE PRINT)
Address	Apt. #
City	State/Prov.	Zip/Postal Code

Signature (if under 18, a parent or guardian must sign)

Mail to the **Harlequin Reader Service:**
IN U.S.A.: P.O. Box 1867, Buffalo, NY 14240-1867
IN CANADA: P.O. Box 609, Fort Erie, Ontario L2A 5X3

Not valid to current subscribers of Harlequin® American Romance® books.

Want to try two free books from another line?
Call 1-800-873-8635 or visit www.morefreebooks.com.

* Terms and prices subject to change without notice. Prices do not include applicable taxes. N.Y. residents add applicable sales tax. Canadian residents will be charged applicable provincial taxes and GST. Offer not valid in Quebec. This offer is limited to one order per household. All orders subject to approval. Credit or debit balances in a customer's account(s) may be offset by any other outstanding balance owed by or to the customer. Please allow 4 to 6 weeks for delivery. Offer available while quantities last.

Your Privacy: Harlequin is committed to protecting your privacy. Our Privacy Policy is available online at www.eHarlequin.com or upon request from the Reader Service. From time to time we make our lists of customers available to reputable third parties who may have a product or service of interest to you. If you would prefer we not share your name and address, please check here. ☐

HAR09R2

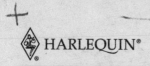

HARLEQUIN®

American ★ Romance®

COMING NEXT MONTH
Available January 12, 2010

#1289 KAYLA'S DADDY by Laura Bradford
Babies & Bachelors USA
When Tate Williams opens his front door, Phoebe Jennings gets the shock of her life! How can the gorgeous bachelor be the recipient of a forty-year-old letter that showed up in her mailbox? And how's the single mom supposed to resist him…especially when he starts bonding with her baby girl? Is fate bringing a decades-old love full circle?

#1290 THE TWIN by Jan Hudson
Texas Outlaws
Sunny Outlaw Payton left the Austin police force for a quiet life running her family's Chili Witches Café. Then in walks Ben McKee, a Texas Ranger who really knows how to turn up the heat! Sparks fly—but the newly widowed Sunny can't fall for another man with a dangerous job in law enforcement. Even if he is the "good guy" her outlaw heart's been searching for….

#1291 BABY MAKES SIX by Shelley Galloway
Motherhood
Four months after Shawn's divorce became final, she realizes she's pregnant with her ex-husband's baby! Juggling the demands of her three young daughters and a busy job, she's not sure she can take another chance on Eddie. Will a new baby magnify their problems…or make them a family again?

#1292 BACHELOR COWBOY by Roxann Delaney
If a little R & R is what it takes for injured rodeo rider Dusty McPherson to return to competition, then a ranch in Desperation, Oklahoma, is where he'll go. But relaxing is the last thing on his mind when he meets beautiful cowgirl Kate Clayborne. Can the stunning redhead convince him that risking his life is nothing compared with risking his heart?

www.eHarlequin.com

HARCNMBPA1209